Blend

The Hummus Series
Book 3

T.K. Richards

To Those That Weather The Storm

Chapter 1
Nadia

My moans woke him. He watched me squirm and trace my inner thighs while I dreamed of his manliness, stroking near the verge of exertion. Deep inside of me. The wind from his nose tickled my neck as I grasped the back of his head, ravenously filled with intensity and gratification, when suddenly Lucas rose from behind me.

His mouth serenaded the small of my back up to the lobes of my ear; his fingers circled my shoulder. And I welcomed him. We welcomed him. Staring deep into Maximus's eyes, I smirked. I was having my cake and eating it, too. No secrets. No sneaking around. Pleasured by the two men who desired me.

Lucas's fingers travelled to my mouth, and I parted my lips to welcome them. The room shook as if it was being hit by an earthquake and faded to black. Then fervent kisses pressed against my cheeks woke me, and the insatiable nightmare came to an end.

My eyes widened, no longer bound by the fantasy of my inner desires, but enthralled in the reality of it about to happen.

The man I married felt compelled to act without being asked. Grunting in my ear, "Your nipples pierced my back and woke me," he said.

He slid my hands from between my thighs. "Allow me," he said, smiling as he spread my slit and felt my heat. "Look how wet you are for me. Waiting patiently for your wakeup call."

I lured him in closer, rolled on top of him and said, "Then give it to me."

I didn't require a taste, but I was in the mood to taste him. His morning wood upended in the air through the opening on his briefs. My lips kissed it. "Good morning," I said before placing his cock in my mouth.

The sound he makes whenever my lips grip his shaft emboldens me, so I worked them upward until he shook and nearly lost his mind. I had become accustomed to pleasing him. Over the past few months I did a lot of pleasing and giving. Partially because of the guilt filled stint in New York, punishing me mentally. But also, because of the power I felt when I made him feel like a King. The way every man wants to feel.

Now that I was free from the burden of fear, and trusting him wholeheartedly, I breathed for the first time in years. I stopped holding back in our marriage, tried a few new things, and gave **ALL** of myself to him. *'It took me some time to get here, but finally I had arrived.'*

I caught a whiff of chlorine as the taste of salt pierced my tongue, so I retreated, careful not to cheat myself if I didn't hold back. Maximus suffered from my withdrawal and quickly mounted me, aware how badly I needed him to start my day off proper.

With full aggression and the right precision, the pressure of his circumference punctured his way to ecstasy. Uncontrollable pleasure took over my body and my mind, and a yearning for more throbbed between my thighs.

Mr. Sharper gave me what I wanted, and the aftershocks of his morning pillage were equally as hot as the steam from the shower. I smiled to myself in the mist, still feeling the work he put in, until the reverie of Mr. Fleming flashed before me, and wiped the smile from my lips.

As the water soaked my skin, the image of Mash, myself, and Lucas sharing a bed puzzled me. It was nice, but puzzling. I veered off into a daze, searching for reasons why he invaded my dream when I hadn't thought about him in months. *'Why rise from the crypt of my mind now?'*

Forgetting to lather the back of my body, the mistakes I made in New York rushed back to me: the motorcycle, the private lunch, the farewell letter, the first kiss, and the last. What I thought I buried across the ocean was wrapped in guilt, hurling about inside, now haunting me in exotic twisted dreams.

I fully regrouped and dressed before the morning rush was upon me. I saw Mash off and turned on my laptop for a virtual call with Yohan. Once our session ended, I dug into my latest edits for our second project, then met Olive on her side of town for a yoga class.

Conversation between us was light this morning. The most we chatted was during downward dog when the instructor couldn't see our mouths move. Then after class we scheduled a time to grab lunch, as both of us were in a hurry to tend to our mates.

I grabbed a salad from the market, and ingredients for a romantic dinner to reset the mood for an instant replay of the morning pillage. While massaging steaks, slicing potatoes, and slaving over the stove, I pictured Mash's perfect hard on pounding me into oblivion on the staircase.

It was our first night back from the states, and we were still riding high from Shannon's wedding weekend. The exhaustion from travel somehow disappeared once we landed, and we fucked like rabbits between, and on top of boxes stacked throughout the apartment. But the way we finished on the stairwell was epic.

I had him pinned against the rails howling, "Nadia, I fucking missed you!" He was helpless as I sucked on his cock like a banshee under his guidance with my hair in his fists. He liked that. Truth be told, I liked it, too. I was making up for the months I abandoned him, and the nights we spent apart before my departure. Just thinking about that night had me ready for him to come home. *'Yeah, I'm going to jump him as soon as he walks in the house.'*

Lost in my memories, the timer on the stove ticked, and the door from the garage slammed. I somehow missed hearing it lift on the other side of the house. Mash called out to me in a rage, "Nadia, where are you!?"

"Follow the aroma!" I shouted, whipping the potatoes into cream.

Mash entered the kitchen brooding and upset, but I did what came naturally, and flashed my teeth whenever I saw him. He didn't reciprocate. Instead, his face tensed, his eyes twitched, and he lifted a yellow package in one hand, and a flip phone in the other and asked, "Who the fuck is Lucas Fleming?"

Chapter 2
Nadia

I damn near dropped my prongs in the oven when Mash said his name. I glanced at the phone then back to him, afraid to breathe, blink, or speak. A rush of blood ran to his head and the package vibrated from his trembling hands.

My silence made the situation worse. My voice rattled, spewing unknown sounds as my lips formed to pronounce words but failed. My mind lost function, until it became clear last night's erotic nightmare was a warning.

I closed the oven, and answered his question with a question. "Lucas Fleming from New York?" Mash stood in silence with a blank expression on his face. I cleverly added, "He is a guy I met who gave me a list of the best places to visit before I left the city. Why do you ask?"

"He sounds like he gave you more than a list." His tone berated me.

I raised my brows. "What are you saying?"

"I'm saying there's something you're not telling me. There are over a hundred messages on this phone addressed to you for fucks sake!" He kicked the floor board.

"Okay, you need to calm down. You're getting way ahead of yourself. All this guy did was offer insight into the city. I wouldn't give him my number, so he insisted I take the phone you're holding to tell me about the latest happenings and special events. As you can see I sent it back to his office. As you can hear from his messages, I didn't communicate with him. End of story. Think! I honestly don't know how or why it was sent here." My chest ached with fear and guilt.

"It has a return to sender stamp on it. The building in New York forwarded it here. What aren't you telling me?"

I sighed and rested my hands on the counter. I couldn't look at his face covered in hurt and anger. "What are you accusing me of?" I asked, searching for a way to make this conversation end.

He scoffed and roamed the floor. "Nadia, did you cheat on me while you were in New York?"

"No. Why would you think that?"

"Because I'm holding a fucking phone with a man's voice begging my wife to call him!"

The phone flew across the kitchen as I screamed. "Stop yelling at me! I didn't have an affair! Jesus, Mash. You had a key to the apartment, and we talked all the fucking time."

His eyes cut me down and his voice cracked. "I'm going to ask you one final time, and I want the truth. Did you fuck this man?"

'Only in my dreams.'

"I said no! Go somewhere and cool off. We can discuss this later." I reached for the spatula and dropped it in the pot of potatoes.

"I don't believe you." He paused. "You need to leave."

"Excuse me?" I frowned at him.

"I want you out," he said with venomous eyes.

"Mash, be mindful of your words. There is no going back

from certain things, and those words in particular I take person-ally," I said.

"You want me to be mindful of my words when you were... Humph, that's rich. I want you to take whatever you want and get the fuck out of my house! Tonight!" he shouted, and flung the canisters from the countertop to the floor.

I shook and held my chest, staring at him with the devil in his eyes. Red with heat and poisonous darts aimed for me. I had witnessed his temper, but never like this—And never with me.

I recalled when we met, he told me, "I say what I mean, and I mean what I say." And he meant those words. *'Get the fuck out of* **MY** *house!'*

I stood at the stove, frightened. Afraid to make a move. I waited for him to retract his statement. Say he was sorry for shouting at me. Apologize for losing his head.

The final timer for dinner buzzed, killing the silence between us. "Mash," I called out to him.

He turned around, fanned me off, and left me standing in my stupidity.

I died on the inside from the way he looked at me, and my heart broke when he fanned me off. It felt as though he was treating me like a fly and told me to *shoo*, or as he would say, "Bugger off."

What I had done in the dark came to the light, screwing me over tenfold. I hadn't thought about Lucas since I safely made it out of New York, yet he found a way to disrupt my happiness. But I couldn't put all of the blame on him. *Fucking guilt.*

I refused to allow a meaningless kiss to uproot my life. A kiss I stopped because I knew the hurt it would bring. A kiss I used to say goodbye and end an affair before it ever started.

I would not be dismissed from the man who constantly professed his love to me, and in an instant wrote me off. Feeling sick throughout my skin, I followed him, and begged him to listen. "I did not cheat on you. Do you hear me?" I pushed on his heels.

Mash shut the door to the studio and locked it behind him. I banged on the door, shouting through the oak, "Are you being serious right now! You know damned well I wouldn't do that to you!"

I pressed my face against the door. A loud thump, followed by glass shattering created a forceful vibration. I cautiously jumped back as music blasted from the other side. I held my chest and fell to the floor, whimpering silently for at least ten minutes. I thought, 'Surely, *he would check on me and take back those vicious words.*'

He did not. The music never settled, and the studio door never opened. Distance grew between us a mile a minute. Angrily I pushed back to the kitchen, tossed the meal I labored over in the garbage, then heaved on top of it. When my stomach settled, I made my way to our bedroom and stood in front of the fireplace.

I cased the décor from wall to wall, unsure if I should pack my bags. The new house felt like my home, and I grew furious at the thought of leaving it after finally settling in. Six weeks of shopping, and ordering, and measuring and designing—all for nothing. Lost over a fucking kiss.

I sat on the edge of the bed and waited for Mash to calm down and talk to me. My nose dripped and my head ached, but I waited. And waited. One full hour went by and nothing.

Feeling silly and desperate, I lazily packed one bag. I didn't organize or select what went inside my luggage. Whatever my hands touched I threw inside, and the more I fumbled through the hangers, the more I became filled with rage. I stopped using suitcases and threw arm loads of clothes, purses, and shoes in the back of my SUV— filling every inch of the car to the point I couldn't see out of the windows.

I sat in the garage, still waiting for Mash to face me and say anything. "Sorry, don't leave," "I didn't mean what I said," "I love you." Anything to stop the pain burning in my chest. The longer I held out for reconciliation, it became clear he wasn't coming to check on me or make amends.

I pulled out of the garage and drove to the end of our street, put the car in park, and heaved again on the side of the road. My neighbors having a late evening run tended to me, offering to escort me back home. I lied to them moments after I composed myself. "My husband isn't home. I'll be fine driving myself to the ER."

I exited the gate, hoping to see Mash's silhouette appear in my rearview window, running to catch me like a scene from a movie. Wishful thinking on my part that didn't happen.

I sighed and slowly drove away from the neighborhood into the dark streets with nowhere to go. I roamed until I grew tired, finally stopping at a hotel I would normally never stay in. But the night was far from normal.

I checked into the lodging, unable to wrap my head around what was happening. I bounced from the chaise to the bed, holding myself while my mind ran itself crazy. Thinking of him, of us, and what was supposed to be— Crying in between the good and bad memories flashing before me.

Sometime in the night I made my way under the covers, and when the sun rose I was already awake, shaking in the poorly made lumpy structure. My eyes were swollen, and my hands shuddered in my mouth as I bit off my fingernails. My chest hurt as if I had been hit by a car, and my insides felt like a roller coaster. Waves of pain and quivering aches traveled through my body, and they were all too familiar. I had been here before. Dylan emerged from the hate pile of my thoughts — though this time I felt ten times worse -- and from there I blacked out.

With no master plan, backup plan, or indication what my next move was going to be, I foolishly assumed we were solid. And though I had money in my possession, I was clueless and lost without Maximus Sharper being a factor in my decision making.

Depression found its home in my mind once again. It seeped into its familiar corner, bringing with it the pain that flowed through my veins, weakening my body. I could barely move to wipe my tears soiling the bedding, and found myself held up in the low budget motel, sleeping incessantly from despair.

Every morning I beat the sun rising, until days later I accepted my time abroad had come to an end. I boxed my clothes from the car, and moved them into a storage unit near Olive and Yohan's house. I gave Olive the key to check on my belongings until I returned, and begged her to keep quiet about my dilemma.

She gave me her word and arranged for Mervin, their driver, to deliver me to the airport in style. I hesitated getting out of the car. My legs shivered, and my breathing skipped. Olive patiently consoled me in the drop off zone, and offered her cottage in France as a temporary getaway until I was ready to face reality.

Exhaling deeply, I declined and pretended I didn't experience a panic attack in front of her, though my flushed face told a different story. My words pacified my true feelings, and I convinced her the best place for me was home. "Call me if you need anything. Anything." She emphasized with a stern look in my direction.

"I will. I promise I won't be a stranger." I smiled.

"Now go let off some steam and find that pretty girl I was jealous of that *one* time."

We cackled hard at the first joke I ever heard her tell. She hugged and released me, then I bravely stepped on the console and faced my reality. I was done in London.

With nothing but time and space to comfort me in the air, I reflected on the past two and a half years. The night at the club where I met Mash, my work with Yohan, my friendship with Olive, the hate I felt being caught between her and Shannon, and then Lucas. The night I met him replayed over and over in my head until I became annoyed with myself.

I did my best to spin the truth, and pinned the blame solely on Lucas and not myself. I faulted Chili for inviting me out the night I met him. I faulted Shannon for answering the phone the night we went to his place. And in the end, I blamed the real villain. Me. I shouldn't have gone to the bar, and I should have tossed his business card out of the window, or left it in the back-seat of the cab.

My sulk-fest lasted throughout my flight. By the time I landed in New York for a three-hour layover into Charlotte, I conjured the nerve to confront Lucas and thank him for ruining my life. I headed toward the exit with the burning question mouthing on my lips. *'Why did you do a return to sender with that godforsaken phone? Did you think I would want you after ruining my life?'*

As bad as I wanted answers to my questions, I cowered and listened to the voice speaking to me in my head. *'Don't go. Don't let his plan work.'*

I turned around and headed back to my gate, spinning out of control. Thriving off of impulse, I turned off my phone and changed my plans, purchasing a one-way ticket from a random counter, and ended up in Cincinnati.

Boarding the flight was better than sitting in JFK for three hours with the itch to seek out Lucas. The spontaneity of being wild as the wind increased my pulse, and spared me the embarrassment of returning home with my tail between my legs for a while. I was sure wagers were made of how long Mash and I would last. But I bet they never thought I would be the one to screw it up.

I landed in Ohio as a lost soul with nowhere to go, or direction of what to do. Following the other travelers to the turnpike, I hailed a taxi. "Take me to the nicest hotel in the city," I said.

As my luck would have it, the hotel the cabbie drove me to had availability. I made myself comfortable in a deluxe room where I ordered movies, and loaded up on room service, pinching from every plate delivered until boredom struck me. When eating became sickening, I entertained my sorrows at the lobby bar. Whatever the server suggested, I taste-tested and ordered until my vision became blurry.

The staff saw to it I returned to my room unscathed. It was way past noon when I woke with a hangover from hell, leading to my second day in town being spent in bed.

The next day I took recommendations from the hotel concierge and agreed to go on a tour of the city. *'Please let this sightseeing excursion help clear my head.'*

It didn't. As the guide read the history of sites such as the National Underground Railroad Freedom Center, Spring Grove Cemetery & Arboretum, and Taft Museum of Art, I managed to be at ease. But when she began talking about the novels based in Cincinnati, a sadness overwhelmed me. A brief mention of Toni Morrison's *Beloved* caused me to tear up, and melancholy knocked me on my ass when we arrived at Eden Park. "The famous novel *The Ghosts of Eden Park* is all about this place," she said.

It dawned on me as we toured the grounds, I was a single amongst couples. How I missed that fact on the bus, verified I wasn't in the proper head space to be amongst people.

The guide continued to read from her script, but her narration was no match for my emotions erupting in public. I turned into a mental patient, sitting at the back of the trolley, while the others continued to stroll in the park.

Unable to hide my tears behind my sunglasses, I softly wept in my corner of the carriage. The passengers took turns looking back at me. Few offered their help. "I'm fine," I lied. "I just learned of some bad news."

I suffered amongst them until the next stop, hailing a taxi back to the hotel. Humiliated and ashamed, I spent the rest of the day locked inside my room, repeating my drunken sorrow fest.

How unwise, drinking on an empty stomach. I paid for that mistake dearly over in the night. Migraines and stomach cramping painfully sobered me up, as the bed hugged me throughout the next morning and afternoon.

When the moon flew high in the sky, I took my bucket of tears to the airport and left Ole Cincy.

While standing in line to buy a one-way ticket home to Charlotte, I had a change of heart. Las Vegas called out to me.

I always dreamed of seeing the Grand Canyon as a little girl, but as a not so poor, not so middle-class family of four, such a trip was considered a luxury. Twenty years later, I was finally able to see the magic—alone on a helicopter tour, snagging a cancellation in two days.

The forty-eight hour wait presented me with time to unwind and be still. And this time, I regrouped without alcohol and a personal goal to not embarrass myself further in public.

While searching for my sanity, I took advantage of the hotel's amenities, splurging on a full day at the spa:

a facial, mani and pedi, body exfoliation, and a massage to relieve the knots of tension in my neck. The healing stones allegedly removed the negative energy, and cleared the rancid thoughts in my head. *'Temporarily.'*

I woke up the next morning rejuvenated, browsed in the

boutiques in the hotel, and dined in one of the many eateries. Money and food were wasted yet again, as my appetite still hadn't returned, and another memorable meal was packed in a box to sour in my room.

To finish off the day, I rented a car and drove out to Area 51, curious to see what the hype was all about after watching a program of conspiracy theories on a local channel. The drive and the views of the mountains along the way briefly cleared my head. But the closer I drove to the sight, and read the danger and warning signs with the monotonous scenery of the red desert in the backdrop, disturbing images entered in my head.

I daydreamed I ignored the do not cross sign and jumped over the government-controlled fence. Bullets blew through me and put me out of my misery. Envisioning my death woke me from the horrid, dark fantasy, and I jerked the car to the side of the road.

Huffing and gasping for air, I teared up at the image of me lying lifeless in the dirt. *'I'm sad but not that sad. I don't think.'*

I drove back to the city, cursing myself for being dumb and weak, slapping the steering wheel to release my frustration. My body shivered, and my eyes watered continuously along the drive. I needed help. But not therapy help. I required check in a hospital and become sedated help.

Once the car was safely returned to the airport, I hopped the hotel shuttle, and relaxed on the feather stuffed mattress. Sleeping until the alarm woke me the next morning.

The helicopter ride to Arizona lifted off, and alas I was up in the air viewing the red and russet colored rocks of the canyon. The formation of grooves took my breath away, reminding me of Es Vedra in Ibiza. A single tear fell down my cheek, this time accompanied with a smile. The love I felt in that moment filled me from head to toe, and remembrance of those emotions somehow pacified me.

My veneration of the canyon soothed my aching soul, then the magic happened. We rode in the flat of the ravine during sunset and an unexpected, indescribable feeling came over me. I didn't know how to receive it or explain it, but I felt the presence of energy embrace me, and a sense of serenity took over my thoughts.

Something spoke to me and said, "Everything is going to be alright." I laughed to myself, thinking of the good times I shared with Mash, and also realized I had an interest in geology. I scoffed. *'My aha moment.'*

Here I was thirty years old, learning something of nature was important to me, as it guided me back to my true self. Back to me.

I felt anew and less dejected as the chopper flew back to Las Vegas, somehow balanced and filled with courage to finally fly home to Charlotte the next morning, ready to begin the healing process.

Chapter 3
Lucas

I ransacked my office, the mailroom, and my secretary's desk like a madman. *'Where the fuck is Nadia's package? I have the note, but what good is it without the phone? She could be calling me right now. Dammit! It has to be in here somewhere.'*

I couldn't get her off of my mind. She left me on edge like a message left on read and the three dots stopped moving— With no way to find her. No last name. No address. Nothing. *'How could I lose the one thing that could connect us?'*

A woman had never had such a lasting effect on me. I sat in my office for weeks imagining she waltzed through the door with those luscious plum lips slightly parted, and lured me over to sink into my arms. Every day the dream added something new to fill the void. No longer did I only envision her supple lips. Soon her breasts and mahogany nipples became clear, and real, and they were perfect, begging for me to kiss them. Then I'd wake just as my lips opened to taste her flesh. Hard as steel about to burst through the seams of my pants. *'God I hope she returns and puts me out of my misery.'*

For days I held my breath, waiting for the day to be graced by her beauty. We had something special, I know it. And in my mind, Nadia belonged with me. *'She will be mine.'*

The women I've dated couldn't light a candle to her. Her mysterious ways would keep any man guessing, and her resiliency and restraint disturbed my rest for many nights. Most of the girls I've encountered, begged for me to please them after seeing my endowment. But not Nadia. She wasn't a whore like most of the women I've slayed.

If I'm honest with myself, I fell for her the moment she sat next to me at Al's. I knew then I found what I had been searching for, but her stupid husband stood in my way. Never having met the guy, I knew he couldn't possibly treat her the way she deserved to be treated. If he did, she wouldn't have been alone in the city spending time with the likes of me.

———

Two months passed, and no sign of her. I gave up and accepted I would never see Nadia again. My memory of her was the only piece of her I'd ever have since the package was never found, and the phone was lost.

Out of frustration and despair, I burned her note in my sink causing the smoke alarm to sound. As I fanned the flames, I read her aching words for the final time:

*'Leave this phone number in service.
It might ring one day.'*

Her words gave me false hope, yet I wondered if she thought about me the way I thought about her—from the moment I wake, throughout the day, to whatever hour I passed out at night. The only way I would know is if she appeared before me. And I waited for that day.

To distract me of my agony, I took on new projects and worked day and night. My days were long, filled with investors and long pocket clients with the capital gains to expand my company's brand.

A newcomer to the city with big ideas on my calendar got me out of bed early one morning. I needed the diversion and the account. A big project with a mogul financially fit to take risks could have helped me restore my image in the office after months of outbursts and erratic behavior.

Normally, clients traveled with at least two representatives for the first summit, but my assistant escorted one gentleman into my office. 'Strange,' I thought, expecting a team. I readjusted my pitch to the well-groomed gentleman standing opposite me across the desk with a serious demeanor, reeking of wealth.

I raised my hand to shake his and he refused. Again, catching me off guard. I cleared my throat and retrieved my hand. "Please have a seat." I gestured to the seat next to him. He unbuttoned his blazer and sat, staring at me viciously.

Wasting no more time, I began to sell the vision my partners and I discussed for the property in question when he abruptly interrupted me. "Scrap all of the plans you had in mind. I'll keep it brief. I'm here to advise you to stay away from my wife," he said.

"I'm sorry. I don't follow," I replied. My brows raised to my forehead in bewilderment. "I have no idea what you're talking about. Whom, may I ask, is your wife?"

"You prey on that many, *huh?* When's the last time you spoke to Nadia?" His eyes narrowed in on me.

And there it was. The name of all names to shatter me into pieces. When Nadia said my money didn't matter to her, I understood why. It was chump change compared to this family's generational wealth.

My research team found files on an older Mr. Sharper, who must be this guy's father, and who I was expecting to meet with. My net worth couldn't compete with this family, and judging by his suit, I had my work cut out for me.

I figured he'd only come to see me because there was trouble in paradise. I crafted my response carefully after staring at Nadia's husband with a grin on my lips. "So, you're the one standing in my way," I answered.

"You're the one who can't move me." He huffed.

"So Nadia's last name is Sharper?" I smirked.

"Mrs. Maximus Sharper to be exact," he bragged, tugging on his lapel as if his words intimidated me.

"To answer your question, I haven't seen Nadia in several months. How is she?" I asked, intentionally to agitate him.

"Humph. It seems you are a bit of a beggar, Mr. Fleming," he said, pulling out the missing flip phone from his pocket.

My eyes grew big, and the veins in my temple inflated. "The missing piece," I said, surprised to see it in his possession.

He laughed a rich man's laugh as if he pitied me. "A flip phone? Really? What kind of company gives their employees flip phones these days? And what kind of desperate man gives it to a woman who is clearly not interested?"

"Nadia does play hardball, but I wouldn't say isn't interested."

"Watch yourself carefully when referring to my wife, Mr. Fleming." His nostrils flared and his face turned flushed pink.

"What exactly can I do for you. Mr. Sharper?" I reclined in my chair and folded my arms.

"It's simple. Stay away from my wife. And don't ever try to contact her again."

"You seem nervous, Mr. Sharper. Trouble in paradise?" I laughed.

"You'd like that, wouldn't you? Unfortunately for you, my wife and I have a bond most couples don't achieve. I'm sure she's spoken of her loyalty to me, or did you not talk while you were shagging her?"

"She did mention something about her devotion to you, but unfortunately it wasn't while I was fucking her. If I had, she'd still be in New York. I mean, she wanted me to give her the goods, but you got in the way. I did, however, taste those succulent lips of hers, but again, you got in my way. It's a damn shame, too. I never got the chance to butter my potato, but I think that may be changing soon, once I find her— Thanks to you. I appreciate you stopping by and giving me what I needed. I finally have a name to put with the face. Nadia Sharper." I dragged her name to taunt him.

I pushed the button I wanted to push. He stood as if he was about to leave, but sucker punched me. He adjusted his jacket as if I was going to sit there and not retaliate. I sneered at him acting like he was the big man on campus, and shook off the blow, then rose to my feet. "If you fuck the way you hit then you've already lost, my friend."

He charged me with another blow I didn't see coming. He south-pawed me, and I had to give it to him— He was swift. I could feel the rage in that hit and rightfully so. I knew Nadia was holding honey in her Cheerio, and her husband was fighting to keep her sweetness away from me.

I stepped out of my professionalism and swung to return a lick; but he took a step back, causing me to send wind in his direction.

"If you fuck the way you miss I have nothing to worry about, my friend. Let this be the last time we meet," he said, and strolled out of my office.

I had never been more infuriated or annoyed by another man in my life. He ignited a fire in me I hadn't felt since my early days of bar fights in the city.

He also made me want his wife even more. I could already taste her sweet nectar on my lips. Feel her supple skin pressed against mine. Her ample ass in my palm. Our union was long overdue, but surely Nadia Sharper was about to be mine.

Chapter 4
Mash

The image of another man's hands on my wife caused my temper to flare, and I threw the phone against the hardwood. I wish it had shattered into pieces like my ego, but I only managed to crack the battery casing and bend the antenna.

I couldn't stand to look Nadia in the face, so I locked myself inside my studio until the morning. And like I demanded, she was gone.

It was the last time I saw her. She was disheveled and scared, and I showed her a side of me that terrified her. I couldn't live with myself knowing I put her in such a frantic state. I also couldn't live with knowing she would betray me and take a lover, especially after learning about my past.

She knew how damaged I was from the deceit Senior and Nomi caused me. *'How could Nadia hurt me like this?'*

With her gone, I was stuck with the memory of her bawling her eyes out uncontrollably on the floor, when I promised I would love her forever. A total hypocrite I proved to be.

'What the bloody hell was wrong with me? Why didn't I

believe her?' A man knows when his woman has let another play in his house, and I knew Nadia loved me enough to never violate my trust, or allow another to destroy what we had. I should have listened to her, but I didn't, and now I've lost her.

Three days passed, and she hadn't turned up. I barged into Yohan's office making an ass of myself, demanding he call Olive and question what she knew. He denied my request, and I couldn't blame him. I was out of line and would have denied him the same if he'd acted as I had.

Frustrated and embarrassed, I apologized with my head up my ass. Han offered to notify me if he heard anything. We shook hands, and he patted my shoulder sympathetically. "Women. What can you do?" he said, shaking his head.

Nightfall was upon me as I sat at my low point of despair. When my phone rang, I answered on the first ring, hoping it was her. It wasn't. "Olive drove Nadia to the airport, but doesn't know where she was heading," said Yohan.

"Has she heard from her since her departure?"

"She has not. I'll touch base if I hear anything," Han promised.

My Nadia was gone. A waif somewhere out in the world alone. Unreachable and unattainable, and it was my fault.

The suspense of her whereabouts drove me insane. I called her phone numerous times, receiving her voicemail on the first ring. The laugh in her greeting stole a piece of my soul, but I dialed her number incessantly to hear her voice. I needed her to know how sorry I was for my behavior. For my words. How disgusted I was with myself for not believing her.

Wanting to apologize in person, I only breathed when the line beeped to speak. My body ached, but I feared she was in more pain from my verbal blows. I longed to hold her in my arms and beg for her forgiveness, smell the pomegranate scent in her hair, and taste her delicious lips to heal my open wound. *'I should have never told her to leave.'*

The days rolled into a week with no word from Nadia. Her absence destroyed me. Her unknown whereabouts led me to the edge of my sobriety and on the brink of buying an eighth to have a minute of peace. Four years off the white, and there I was remembering only the good it did me. The brief high and gift of blissful short moments of not giving a fuck about anything. *'Don't do it,'* I convinced myself.

She left me no choice but to track her phone. When New York appeared on the screen, my insides damn near fell to the floor. *'If I've run her into that wanker's arms I will kill myself,'* I thought. I threw her to the wolves, but couldn't fathom the thought of never getting her back. It would truly be the biggest mistake of my life.

Before Nadia left, she wanted me to reconnect with my father. Her disappearance led me to his doorstep. Forcing me to make amends with the man I despised. I went to him and asked to use his resources and connections to locate her as I had failed. He sensed the severity of my need, and didn't torture me with questions. A simple nod, and it was done. "One more thing," I added. "Find out what you can about a Lucas Fleming in New York."

He nodded. "I'll call you when I have something, son."

Senior called me son as if he had been waiting years for the right time to use it. I denied myself to find joy in the moment, and headed over to Prano's place to ask for a favor.

He made a run to the yard for me, and I left without explanation. I took my package, contemplated throwing it out of the window on the drive home, but the addict in me wouldn't let it slip from my fingers. Tiny bits of sweat formed with it in my palms as I slipped down a slippery slope I swore to never skate on again.

It comforted me back at the house, where I walked room to room, haunted by Nadia's ghost. Her spirit watched me make the tragic mistake of reacquainting my nose with candy, searching for a moment of relief.

I lied back on the couch and thought I felt her climb on top of me. I smiled at the thought she'd forgiven me and come home, and I imagined I pressed my lips against hers. For a moment, I was relieved she was back where she belonged. Her supple breasts pressed against me, her flowing hair tickling my chin, her dark brown eyes summoning me to mount her.

The morning I foolishly told her to leave played before me during my flight. Her smooth, perfect dark skin glowing in the stream of moonlight which crept through the shutters, while I had her pinned against the sheets. Her curves thrusting up at me, receiving all I had to give. I loved looking at her when we made love. Watching her enjoy every stroke I planted inside. The way her mouth moved when she called my name, and how she slightly opened her lips when she came like she was ashamed. It was as if she held her breath when she climaxed. What a perfect morning we shared. She wanted me before the sunlight hit our window, moaning as she yearned for me in her sleep, and damn near swallowed me whole— sucking me the way I taught her. I loved when she was on one.

Suddenly, her image faded into thin air. I became embarrassed with myself for thinking she was really in the room. I never thought she would see me like this. She didn't know me when I was on blow years ago, and I would never bring her around such disgrace. But her ghost saw me. And that was bad enough.

I sat on the couch and let my high mellow itself out. When I woke, I packed a bag and caught the next flight to New York. I was determined I would find her, and Lucas Fleming was where I started.

I posed as a potential client and had his secretary squeeze me in for an appointment at the end of the week. He was taller than me but posed no threat. I could take him if he tried his luck, plus I had sheer determination to punish him for the trouble he caused.

It took everything in me not to strike him as soon as I entered the room, but I enjoyed his little clown dance— tap dancing for me to earn a buck. The look on his face when I interrupted his spill was priceless, and when he learned who I was, I sensed an urgency of desperation.

He did his best to taunt me with words, claiming he could sit in my seat, but also confirmed there was no indiscretion on my baby's part. But when he disrespected Nadia, I jabbed him in his mouth. He didn't know what hit him. I dazed him and felt my blood rising, waiting for him to talk slick out of his mouth again, and when he did I punched him a second time. *Bloww!*

He rose to his feet ready to tussle, but I moved too quickly for him, dodging his fist. He realized he was no match for me and didn't dare take a second attempt to lunge at me. He stood in his stance and struggled with a final smart remark, so I finished him off and left him holding his jaw. He learned he didn't want any smoke with me.

I left his office kicking myself. "*BOLLOCKS!*" I muttered, agonizing over the biggest mistake of my life. Losing Nadia. The bastard confessed she never laid with him, and rejected his attempt after he violated her sweet lips. And I let her down. I let her go. I pushed her away.

Her disappearance reminded me of her past battles with depression. In a panic I called Senior, hoping he had an update. "Still no sign of her. It's as if she fell off the face of the earth," he said.

"Well, I have no reason to be in New York. Call me when you have word," I replied, and headed to the airport.

With New York being her last known stop, I was sure she ran to this *pissant*. But after learning she didn't swing his way, the strings lessened around my heart. All I had to do was find her and bring her back where she belongs. Next to me. Hopefully, I'd find her in Charlotte. *'I hope I'm still welcome.'*

Chapter 5
Khai

N adia was known for her surprise visits, so when she called and said, "Bring your keys outside," I sprung to the exit.

As always, we hugged when we saw each other, but didn't spend too much time on the sidewalk because the heat was sweltering. Immediately I recognized something was wrong. Showing up out of the blue on my job hauling luggage around. Red flag.

The two of us were kindred spirits, but I didn't pry. I let her beat around the bush for a bit, then showed her to my car to load her luggage. I clocked out early for the day, sensing she needed her friend. "You are just what the doctor ordered. A good reason to use some vacation time," I said.

"And here I thought I was *gonna* have to convince you to play hooky."

As I wheeled us out of the garage, Nadia's face was flushed with tears. She wiped her nose with one hand, and held a burner phone in the other. "What are you doing with one of those?" I asked. "Where is your phone?"

From the corner of my eye I saw teardrops fall onto her blouse. Quickly, I pulled over to the curb, and we sat until she was able to talk. As she cried, I patted her shoulder to console her, and turned the air conditioner on to full blast to cool us off.

Patiently, I waited for her to calm herself and share the reason she uncontrollably sobbed without warning. I suspected it had something to do with Mash, hence the amount of luggage and unplanned visit, but I wasn't prepared for the load she dropped on me.

Hearing the details unfolding from her lips blew me away. I was disappointed in Mash's behavior, and hurt for my friend. Watching her losing her mind was surreal, and the state of hysteria she descended into as she talked broke me into pieces.

The wound was too fresh to offer words of encouragement that would comfort her, so I said what everyone says to someone who is hurting. "Give it time."

I preached, hoping to restore an ounce of faith in her that everything would work itself out in time. She received my words and slightly perked up, but still offered no explanation of why she was carrying a burner.

I passed her a pack of tissues from the glove compartment, and checked my mirrors for the clear to merge back into traffic. She twisted her lips while drying her eyes and nose. "Wait. Hold up," she said, then opened the door to vomit.

My hands covered my mouth and against my stomach. Nadia closed the door and sat back in the seat. "Are you???" I raised my brows. She turned to face me. "I mean you look smaller than I remember but..."

"I'm not pregnant," she interrupted. "Whenever I think about him and realize it's over between us, it comes up. And I didn't pack my medicine," she said, wiping her mouth.

"What medicine?"

"My iron pills. My hemoglobin was a 7 the last time my physician checked."

I shook my head. "First things first. Let's get you healthy. You're staying with me."

"I appreciate the offer, but I have a hotel room reserved. I don't want to stay with anyone," she emphasized.

"This isn't a good time for you to be alone," I argued.

Her face stiffened in seriousness, and her voice lost its normal casual tone. "I also don't want anyone to know I'm here. Understood?"

"You aren't thinking straight. Have you eaten?"

"I try, but I can't. And I know how hideous I look. Can we swing by a store? I need to grab a few things before we go to the hotel. By the way, I made the reservation in your name."

I put the car back in park and stared her up and down. "Why did your luggage have a Vegas tag?"

"I spent this past week in Cincinnati, then Vegas. I finally saw the Grand Canyon. It was divine." She praised with her hands.

"By yourself? Like this? For an entire week?"

She nodded.

"You're all over the place. Let my doctor put you on something for a little while." I held her hand until she jerked it away from my grasp.

"For what?" Nadia argued.

"Anxiety. Depression. I say this with love. You don't look so good. The sudden weight loss, low iron, your marriage. Why would you deal with this alone when you have friends and family who are here for you?"

"Look, I'm not ready to face everyone. This fiasco is embarrassing for me. My heart is broken, and a pill is not going to fix it, Khai. I came to you because I trust you the most. And I need you to do something for me," she said in a higher pitched tone of voice.

"What? Call Mash and talk some sense into him?"

"No, please don't tell anyone I'm here, especially him. I'm going to give you some cash to get me a car."

I stared at her in black disbelief. She stared back at me straight-faced and didn't flinch or blink. The silence in the car became awkward until she pulled a wad of cash from her purse. "Nadia, are you in hiding?" I scowled.

"Sort of, but not really. I doubt Mash is looking for me after the way he treated me, and even if he is I don't want to see him. He can never know how badly he has hurt me. I can't lose that kind of power again to a man." Her voice deepened and her eyes pierced mine.

"Same *ole* Nadia," I huffed. "We all fall down at some point. Even you."

"Just say you'll help me buy myself some time to get my shit together. When I'm ready, I'll face the music. Right now, all I need is your name. I found a place in Atlanta. I'll pay you for a year's rent all up front. Same with the car." Her eyes dilated and scared me.

"Say I agree. What's down there?"

"Work possibly. I'm confident I can land a job writing for someone. If not, I can ask Yohan to make some calls to help me get my foot in the door."

"I can't be a part of this and not tell Brian. You can trust him to keep quiet. But what about your mom? You're nuts if you think she won't know something is wrong."

"She doesn't need to know what I'm dealing with. She'll tell Grams, and they'll both worry, and I don't want them to. This is what I want. Can I count on you?"

I agreed to go along with her cockamamie plan if she let my doctor do a workup. The next morning, she was squeezed in while I plotted how to check her into a mental rehabilitation facility. Not really, but it did cross my mind.

Her tests confirmed her iron level dropped to a 6, she was dehydrated, and also suffering from panic attacks. I begged her to stay with me until she was well, but my stubborn, proud, fragile friend refused. "Your doctor is referring me to a hematologist in Atlanta for an infusion next week, so let's head to that car lot." She bossed me.

I don't like authoritarian Nadia. She was exactly like this when she and Dylan broke up. Running around high strung with a crazed look in her eyes. Then the next minute crying. Then the next minute pretending to be tough. Treating everyone like they owe her allegiance, until she crashes, and someone needed to be with her to pick up the pieces.

As I dealt with the bossy, strong woman persona ordering me around all afternoon, and throwing cash around as if it grew on trees, I waited for her to burn out. She didn't. She test drove and purchased a used sedan in cash, gave me a lump sum for a bank account to use for the rent, and before I knew it we were on our way to Georgia.

We surprised her mother in South Carolina on the way to Operation Disappearing Act. Sadly, I was her accomplice in lying to her sweet mother. I was hopeful Mrs. Melton would see through Nadia's facade, and talk some sense into her. "My Lord, why are you so frail?" Her mother asked when she placed her arms around her.

It took everything in me not to blab. I screamed on the inside. *'Tell her Nadia isn't eating or holding anything down.'*

The good friend in me was torn to keep my word, or abandon our agreement and lose her trust. I held my lips tight.

It sickened me to watch her fib to her mother's face about some made up diet to lose weight for an audition. "I thought you were writing the stories, not acting in them?" Mrs. Melton asked.

"I'm trying to do it all. The women in the industry are toothpicks, so if I am going to compete I have to look like them," Nadia lied. Easily I might add.

'How long has she been planning this charade?'

"Well I don't like it," said Mother Melton.

"Neither do I," I cosigned, and rolled my eyes at Nadia.

Mrs. Melton appeared to buy her daughter's story, but didn't let go of it easily. She scolded Nadia about her weight, and repeatedly placed food in front of the both of us during the visit. She fussed, "I'm upset you girls won't at least spend the night. I can't believe you came all this way, and you can't spend one night with your own mama."

"I'll be back in a few days to spend some time with you. I'm going to hang with the girls this weekend, and then I'm all yours," Nadia promised.

"You better."

Not once did Nadia mention she moved back to the states to her mother. I thought about that during the drive to Atlanta and assumed her pride was controlling her. Her lack of mentioning her return also gave me hope Mash still had a chance to fix this ridiculousness.

Being an accomplice to Nadia's escape made me shaky on the inside, but it didn't stop me from munching on the goodies Mrs. Melton packed for us. Hours later, I signed a twelve-month lease on a townhouse rental. It wasn't the luxurious house in the hills outside London, but at least it was new.

Once we received the keys to the unit, we shopped for necessities during our first night stay. Nadia kept it simple and bought an air mattress and linens, curtains and rods, towels and soap, and a few dishes. She ordered a bedroom and living room set for delivery the next morning, and worked with a burst of energy all evening setting everything into place.

The night reminded me of our college years. "Shit!" Nadia exclaimed. "We forgot to get a TV."

"It would watch us instead of us watching it tonight. I'm tired," I said.

She stood peeping outside from behind the curtains. "If you're having second thoughts, I can break the lease with no problem. You can spend a few days with your mom, or stay with me so you won't get lonely," I offered.

"That won't be necessary. I'll be fine. It shouldn't be too hard to settle back into my old ways of living alone." Her voice withered.

"Has he called you?"

Nadia shrugged her shoulders. "There are a few breathing messages on my voicemail." She sighed.

I was too exhausted to continue trying to break her. I rolled over and went to sleep, awakened in the morning by the delivery workers knocking on the door.

As they set up her furniture, we cleaned the cabinets, the fridge, and bathrooms, then hit the streets for more shopping to spruce up the bare walls.

"Does this remind you of our college days?" she asked.

"I was thinking the same thing last night. Roughing it out with no television in the room."

"Driving down here for the parties." She added.

"And the cute, stupid boys we chased."

"Please don't name them. I've erased those jerks from my memory and want them to stay forgotten forever."

We laughed.

Traveling on a familiar street, we came across our old favorite Mexican restaurant. "You'll be happy to hear this," she said. "I'm hungry."

"Thank God the meds are working!" I shouted.

We sat in a corner off to ourselves. The mariachi sounds over the speaker were loud enough to offer us privacy, and hide the sounds of our stomachs rumbling.

As the smells of the cantina played with our noses, I played twenty questions, testing Nadia's headspace. "How long do you think this little plan of yours is going to work?" I asked.

"Hopefully six months to a year," she said, not batting an eye.

"You are *trippin'* if you don't think Mash is going to find you before then. There is facial recognition technology everywhere. No one has privacy anymore. And he has money. Rich people make things happen."

"The only way he will find me is if someone tells him where I am. My phone is off. He can't track me. I'm using cash only when I need to spend. No one will find me unless I want to be found. Stop believing what you see in the movies."

"You're delusional," I sang in a fun tune. "If this turns into a missing person's case, I will tell your mother everything. And you better cover my ass."

"It won't come to that. Promise you won't mention anything to the girls. Taylor will tell Levi, and he will tell Mash, and he needs to sweat while I prepare how I want to proceed."

"I won't say anything as long as you check in with me so I know you're okay."

Finally, a breakthrough. She turned away from me and wiped a tear forming in her eye. "You don't have to shut out everyone who loves you," I said.

"I have to do this my way," she cried softly. "I can't heal with everyone giving me their opinion, or asking me how I'm doing, or suggesting how to fix this. I want to deal with this privately."

Her eyes watered, and her shirt vibrated heavily near her

chest as she spoke. Somehow, she magically regained her composure. *'Is it strength or determination she is pulling from?'* I wondered.

"Let's talk about something else?" She sniffled and folded her arms.

"It's better to get it out than leave it in. The man loves you. You know that's him breathing on the phone."

"You didn't see how he looked at me." Her voice cracked. "How he sounded, and to tell me to get the fuck out was..." She took a deep breath. "You know how I feel about those words."

I nodded. "Yes, I remember."

"The fairytale is over, Khai. He threw me away like trash. Maybe I am tra..."

"Stop it. You are not trash."

Nadia stared out of the window, still able to control the water glistening in the corner of her eyes. I overstepped, "Don't hate me for asking you this, but have you talked to Lucas?"

"No." Her face scowled at me. "And I don't intend to."

The waiter returned and placed the heavenly scent of refried beans, cumin, and peppers in the center of the table, creating a better vibe between us. We spent the night in the townhouse, then drove back to Mrs. Melton's house in the morning. Brian picked me up from her house, and I slept peacefully in my own bed knowing Nadia was with her mother for a few nights.

As I expected, the secrecy of Nadia's break-up didn't last long. I resisted the urge to call London once the rumor started circling amongst the group. Instead, Brian and I maintained our loyalty and respected Nadia's wishes.

I feared how she would react if she heard the gossip was making its rounds, so I carefully sugarcoated the situation when I checked in with her, days after she left South Carolina. "How are you feeling after the infusion?"

"My legs are a little sore, but I'm not in any pain," she stammered.

"You sound drained."

"I am tired. And in one of my moods."

"Then you're not going to like what I have to say." I briefly paused. "Mash is in town. Have you dialed into your voicemail?"

"No, I haven't. What does he know?"

The sound of panic echoed through the phone from her end. "From what I've gathered, nothing. He showed up in town without warning and met Levi and Brian for drinks. Brian says he is a wreck and got pissy drunk. Levi took him back to his house."

"Fuck! That means Taylor knows."

"So does Shannon. Taylor called the both of us, asking if you were in town and avoiding her. And Shannon shared Yohan called her, questioning if she knew of your whereabouts. They are both on my ass."

Brian walked in the room and stole my attention. "Get dressed. Levi invited everyone over for drinks."

"It's a setup," said Nadia, fuming and gritting her teeth. "Levi and Taylor are getting you all together in one place to snitch."

"I knew he would come looking for you. This is so romantic!" I squealed.

"Um, it's not. He put me out, remember? Keep your *fuckin'* mouth shut. I gotta go." She closed her burner phone violently in my ear.

'I'm going to pretend she didn't hang up on me.'

Chapter 6
Khai

Taylor answered the door and widened her eyes when Brian and I entered. Under her breath she mumbled, "He's real shifty acting," then led us into the living room with the rest of the party.

I greeted Mash. "Just the person I want to see," he whispered in my ear while hugging me. He leaned over to Brian and asked, "Do you mind if I borrow your wife for a second?" Brian gestured his approval, and we eased off into the dining room.

He was good looking, but not looking good. Worry was written in his eyes, and his face appeared lifeless behind his grin. "What are you doing here, and where is my girl?" I asked.

His sad eyes twitched, "I was hoping you knew."

His bottom lip disappeared under his teeth, and he wiped his face with his palms. "So you haven't heard from her?" he asked. I kept my word to Nadia, crumbling at the look of defeat on his face.

"Mash, why don't you know where she is?" I fished.

"I feel like an idiot coming here." He sighed.

"Talk to me. What's going on?" I asked, luring him to tell his side of the story.

"I fucked up. Royally. I lost my temper and told her to leave." He dropped his head.

"No, you told her to get the fuck out." I sneered.

His eyes grew big like the hole inside of a doughnut. "You have talked to her." His face lit like those commercials when a light bulb has gone off in someone's head. "How is she? Where is she? Khai, please? Take me to her now," he begged.

"I can't help you there. She called to check in so no one would worry about her. She said she's going to do a bit of traveling for a while."

"How did she sound? Is she okay?"

"The last time I spoke with her she sounded fine." My stomach twisted. "She says she has her moments, but she's fine."

My shoulders tensed at the look of anguish on his face. I hated lying to him in such a frantic state, and being a part of Nadia's plan to punish him into an early grave. These two belonged together. I knew it from the night I met him at the grunge fest where they put on a shameful public display of affection. I didn't agree with Nadia hiding from him, but I also didn't agree with him throwing her out of their house in the most demeaning fashion either. *I should be lashing out at him right now.*

I opened my mouth to insult him. Then he bit his fist, and his eyes turned watery. His display of self-inflicting pain forced me to hold my tongue. I patted him on the back instead. "Everything will work itself out. I told Nadia to give it time. So, you do the same. In time you two will find your way back to each other. I suggest letting her have her space and let things cool down."

"You think I still have a chance?" His eyes flashed a tiny bit of hope in them.

"Why wouldn't you?"

"Because I accused her of cheating with some prick she met in New York. Khai, he left her so many messages begging her to call him. **My wife**. And when I asked her who he was, she flinched. The way she looked when I called his name tore me apart."

"How did she look?" I pried.

"Guilty. Like she was hiding something."

"Well nothing happened between them. You do know that. Right?"

"I do now. I need to tell her I was wrong, and I'm sorry, and I want her to come home. I need her to come home."

I felt sorry for him. The hopeless romantic in me said drive him to Atlanta, but my loyalty stopped me from betraying Nadia's wishes. "There is something you probably don't know. The words you used have a negative history with Nadia. When we became friends in college, she lived off campus with this girl who couldn't keep a roommate. Long story short, one night they had a disagreement, the girl told her to get the fuck out of her apartment, and because it was in her roommate's name there was nothing Nadia could do but leave. The police were called, the girl threw her stuff all over the lawn, except Nadia's things she chose to keep for herself. She was so distraught, she failed a major test the next day. I came across her crying in the student lounge during my work study. She was looking at the bulletin board when I clocked in, and was asleep on the sofa when I left. The next night, she slept on the sofa in my dorm. Shannon and I moved her into our room, and she crashed on the bean bag for the rest of the semester. She resents anyone who utters those words to her."

"I'm fucked," he mumbled.

"Personally, I think it'll blow over because I know you two are crazy in love, but it's going to take some time. What you also don't know is her ex did this to her as well. She opted out of getting an apartment off campus with us when he convinced her to move in with him. A few months later she found out he was cheating, and he said those very same words to her when she confronted him. She vowed to never live with anyone ever again. Think about how she was hesitant to stay with you."

"I'm kicking myself right now. I have to make this right. Where do you think she is? I'm going to her mother's in the morning. Hopefully I'll find her there."

"You won't. She doesn't want her mom or her Grams to worry. I'm the only person who knows about the separation." My thumb pointed to my chest.

"We're not separated," he emphasized. "How is she calling you?"

"She's traveling with a prepaid phone. I have to wait to hear from her."

"Next time she calls, connect us, please. You have my number. I'm not going back without her."

I nodded, and we rejoined everyone in the living room. I remained sober to avoid a slip of the tongue as the girls eyed me. I knew they wanted to inquire about my private conversation with Mash, but the only person I repeated it to was Nadia, smiling on the other line, pretending not to care.

Chapter 7
Shannon

The jig was up. Something was going on. I knew it when Yohan asked me about Nadia. We've never talked about her before. And when Mash popped up in town without her, it was time Khai was put on Front Street.

She slipped out of the dinner before I could catch her, so I woke Taylor early in the morning and headed over to her house. We rolled up on her doorstep without notice. "Get dressed. We're going to breakfast," I said.

She threw on a pair of leggings and an oversized tee and hopped in the back seat. "Why are we sitting here with the engine turned off?" she asked.

I turned around and locked eyes with her. "I'll start the car when you tell us your secret. What were you and Mash talking about last night? And before you lie, Yohan told me Nadia left him."

She sucked her teeth and looked out of the window. "Well, if you know that much, why are you giving me the third degree?" She stalled.

"Cut the shit, Khai, do you know where she is?"

"I do," she sassed, threatening me with her eyes.

"Why didn't you tell us what was going on?" Taylor asked.

"Because she asked me not to." Khai sighed.

"Well, what happened?" Shannon continued.

"Lucas happened."

"Who is Lucas?" Taylor asked.

"Noooo. I know she didn't leave Mash for him!" I screeched.

"Who is Lucas?" Taylor interrupted.

I turned to Taylor and exhaled, tired of this ordeal, and annoyed at Khai for keeping us in the dark. "Remember when we met for lunch in New York, and I told you and Isla a guy flashed Nadia his penis?"

"Yeah."

"I fudged that story a bit. It was more like he whipped his dick out trying to get some ass and Nadia code *Cailfornia'd* us."

"Ah! Good ole code California," Taylor giggled.

"Nadia didn't leave Mash for Lucas, okay," Khai huffed.

"Did she fuck him?" I inquired.

"No! She didn't sleep with him!" Khai exclaimed. "Yeah, she's too vanilla to do something I would do. But he was tempting if you ask me."

"Let's be clear. No one had sex. Nadia and Mash are in the middle of a serious disagreement. Things got heated, Nadia is on her vengeful trip, and now he's looking for her. End of story."

"I wouldn't leave my house. His ass would have to leave," Taylor chimed in.

I couldn't contain my laughter. The situation wasn't funny, but I imagined Nadia packing up her shit and leaving poor Vanilla Ice clueless. "I'm sorry, but finally getting the details, and thinking about how sad Mash looked last night has me tickled. She's worrying the hell out of that man."

"If he didn't know before, he knows now not to dare a *sistah*," Taylor joked.

"Nadia ghosted him and he's walking around questioning where he went wrong. This shit is classic," I added.

"And we all know Nadia is going to ride this out for as long as she can." Taylor shook her head, smirking.

"We've seen how they're living. She's most definitely going back," I said. "She's probably in New York giving Lucas a whirl right now. Then she'll go back. At least that's what I would do anyway."

The car grew quiet with all of us in deep thought. Taylor broke the silence, "I don't know who this Lucas person is, but I do want to go home, and tell Mash to get the hell out of my house now."

Khai and I snickered. "Go easy on him," Khai suggested.

Taylor turned up her lips.

"So where is Nadia?" I asked.

"I promised not to tell," Khai answered.

Taylor and I gave her the death stare.

"Atlanta."

"Nadia is in party city, and you didn't tell us!" I reached over my seat and pinched Khai.

"Road trip!" Taylor hollered.

"If we all get missing with Mash in town, he is going to know something is up, and last night he said he isn't leaving without her," said Khai.

"With all due respect, his feelings aren't my concern at the moment. Go pack a bag. We'll be back in an hour and ready to ride," I declared.

Mash called Khai during the drive down. Taylor turned down the radio and signaled for her to place the call on speaker. "Have you heard from her?" he asked.

"Not today, no," Khai answered.

Mash grew quiet.

"She is checking her voicemail. Maybe you should leave her a message." Khai proposed.

"I'd rather talk to her directly. If you do hear from her, tell her I love her. I'm checking into a hotel for a few days, hoping she turns up. Call me if you hear anything. Please."

"Will do," said Khai, then sighed once the call ended.

We sat speechless for a while after his sadness transferred into the car with us. "She's really sticking it to his ass," said Taylor. "You sure she didn't cheat?" Khai didn't respond.

The phone call and the silence in the car killed the vibe we had going. To liven things back up, I turned to the radio station we used to listen to whenever we traveled to Atlanta to party. Worked like a charm.

We arrived at an upscale apartment complex north of the city, shy of a four-hour drive. "These units look new, but there is no way Nadia is serious about giving up her life over there to settle for this," I said.

"She must really be pissed at him," Taylor added.

"Before we go in I need to tell you two something. I have seen Nadia, and she didn't look so good. Be nice. Be gentle. And don't judge her when you see her. Okay?" Khai warned us.

We agreed to the terms and stood outside her door with zero conversation happening. Nadia took her time answering the buzzer. I couldn't believe my eyes when she opened the door. My friend with glowing, brown skin and vibrant personality wasn't standing before us. This person let herself go down in the shitter. Her hair hadn't been combed, her appearance was frail, her skin dull and dry, and her spirit defeated.

Normally, I would provide comic relief, but the sight of her rendered my puns and wit. She moved aside and gestured for us to enter. "Yohan spilled the beans. Not me," said Khai.

I followed Khai inside. "Where is my hug?" I asked, grabbing her fragile body.

Taylor came inside behind me. "How are you doing?"

"You be the judge," Nadia answered.

"I don't know what's going on with you, but you'll always be pretty," said Taylor.

Khai and I gasped quietly at Taylor's response. "Maybe there's hope for them after all," I whispered, then followed Khai into the living room. The space was cold, halfway empty, and tragically different from her pad in London. So was our interaction with one another.

After too many awkward silences to count, Taylor broke the ice. "Nadia, this isn't you. Look at your hair, and where did you get this grandma looking track suit you're wearing?" Nadia stared at Taylor with an evil eye, but didn't respond. "Do you have shampoo? I can at least make you look decent until we get you a hair appointment down here," Taylor offered.

Khai and I sat quietly, waiting for Nadia to light into Taylor. She said nothing. "Then it's settled," Taylor announced. "Shannon, go find her something to wear, and Khai give her your hat. We're getting you out of this apartment and putting you back together. This is unacceptable. Let's go, y'all," Taylor ordered.

Khai brushed her hair back into a ponytail, and loaned her hat to Nadia, while I dressed her in a pair of baggy jeans and a tee. We were no strangers to The Peachtree City, our old stomping grounds for parties, and a trail of broken hearts. We knew where to shop and what boutiques to tag.

We pitched in and bought Nadia haircare products, a few cute outfits, and groceries, even though she had more than us in the bank.

To fatten her up, we tried a trendy café and ordered appetizers a la carte, and liquored her up to ease her sorrows. The trick worked, giving her a light buzz. She dug into the plates, moaning over every savory bite. "Is it good?" I asked.

"Um uh," she hummed.

"Did you enjoy today?" Khai asked.

Nadia nodded.

"Now please tell me why Mash is at my house acting all shifty," Taylor blurted.

Nadia placed the chip in her hand back in the bowl of salsa. Khai leaned towards me and whispered, "And you thought they weren't going to bump heads."

The waitress returned with more of our order. Nadia waited for her to leave the table and scoffed. "I appreciate you all coming down here, but I'm fine. Really. I may not look the part. But I'm dealing with this my own way. If you don't want Mash in your house, put him out. He has no problem doing it."

"Nadia, I have to know. Did you sleep with *ole* boy in New York?" I asked.

"Nope, but I should have."

It was hard to tell if she meant that, or if the liquor was talking. "You still can," I said.

"I don't want to." She burped and giggled. "Why don't you sleep with him? At least one of us will have been on that ride to make this all worth it."

'*It's definitely the liquor talking.*'

"You did say he had a weapon of mass destruction. Why pass up the chance to get some decent action when technically, it's owed to you now?" I suggested.

"Then I wouldn't be any better than you and Han?"

I smirked at her smart-ass comment and nodded my head at her verbal dagger. "You still *gotta* problem with that I see. You and Miss Thang must have gotten close over there."

Nadia huffed and turned her head away from me.

Khai intervened. "It's been two weeks, and your husband is

calling me nonstop. He's sorry. And he loves you. Can you at least call him?"

Nadia shook her head no. "I'm starting to make my peace with it. Getting out of the house today did me some good. I admit, I lost control this week because everything was going wrong."

"Like what?" Khai asked.

"Like I fell asleep and missed an application deadline. That led to a crying spell. Then I got a note from the complex manager that my music was too loud. Then I stupidly went for a walk at night, got chased by a dog, fell and scraped my knee. I haven't been out of the house since. Go ahead and laugh. I can laugh about it now since the damned dog didn't bite me."

What began as snickers turned into a roar. Our cackling put the first smile on her face since we arrived. "I wish I could have seen you outrunning a dog!" I hollered.

Nadia finally laughed. Seeing her light up eased the tension and mood, and gave us the clearance to speak freely like we normally do. "How long are you going to punish that poor man?" I asked.

"Whose side are you on?" Nadia rolled her eyes.

"Yours, of course. But you know your life over there was better than this. I mean is Lucas worth coming back to live like us common folk?"

"Lucas has nothing to do with what is going on in my marriage."

"No shade, but I think you liked this Lucas person more than you're letting on," Taylor stated. "And it's okay. It happens. You're married. Not dead."

"I enjoyed the flirtation. That's it." Nadia scowled.

I chimed in. "Lucas liked her. He definitely wanted to hit it, but the question remains, would he have quit it?"

Back at the apartment, Taylor shampooed and braided

Nadia's hair into a bun. She twirled around the room, showing off the finishing touches, and we applauded her fresh look before streaming movies and teasing each other.

Nadia fell asleep before the credits rolled, snoring, wheezing, and grunting—getting the rest she badly needed. Hearing her exhausted pipes saddened the three of us. Our eyes shifted around the room, speaking without words, mutually feeling her sorrow.

"Nobody looks like that after a breakup if they didn't love the person," I whispered.

"I hope she forgives him," said Khai.

Taylor sneered, "Yeah right. Nadia and forgiveness are like oil and water."

Khai and I giggled. If anyone knew what it was like to be on the receiving end of Nadia's wrath, it was Taylor. "I bet you thought she'd never forgive you?" I asked.

Taylor exhaled, "Has she forgiven me?"

The three of us wrinkled our faces at each other, unable to answer Taylor's query, and ended the night with the flaming question in mind. *'Has she really forgiven Taylor, and what did that mean for her and Mash?'*

Chapter 8
Nadia

Once again it was silent. With the girls gone, I was reminded of my loneliness. Stuck with my pride and racing thoughts, I followed Khai's suggestion, and dialed into my voicemail.

It was filled to capacity with his voice. I saved and replayed the messages saying, "*I love you,*" and "*Please call me,*" and "*Come home,*" but the messages with shrill silence and no words, I felt the most. Desperate, jarring breathing, and regret transcending through the quietness.

All night I tossed and turned, waiting for the sun to rise. As I stared at the ceiling fan, I considered my next moves, then I heard his voice call my name. My mind was playing tricks on me, but I found comfort in the prank and welcomed it, happy to reminisce about the morning of the day I left.

I could taste the food I cooked for him, which never made it to my mouth. I felt the sex injuries that were worth the sting in my bones—a minor bruise in the small of my back from the bathroom sink, and a carpet burn on my knees from the studio floor. I also felt my pussy throb thinking of the erotic nights we created.

One night, I told Mash to blow his ganja while I blessed him with my best lip service to date. He looked so damn sexy as his mouth released puffs of thick circles, telling me I would be the death of him as he almost blew my head off. *'Why did I have to be so stupid?'* I wondered, before drifting off.

It was nearly three weeks, seventeen days to be exact, since I saw him last. The dry heaves and panic attacks stopped, but the loneliness continued to occupy my every breath. I was nine pounds lighter, living in a temporary condo in my third city in over two years. *'I never saw any of this coming.'*

As daylight cast a shade of beige in my bedroom, I opened my eyes and couldn't move. Just like the morning I learned I was anemic. As if turning thirty wasn't bad enough, my knees were starting to feel the strain of high heels, and my health decided to add a low blood disorder in the mix.

To top it off, I was a total fucking mess mentally. Not just physically. I was unemployed, newly single, surrounded by strangers, and comfortable with self-loathing.

Haggard and restless, I reported to the doctor's office. The nurse stuck me, filling my veins with the second injection of oxblood and black colored iron. I sat with her for half an hour to make sure I felt fine, then dropped by an electronics store for a new laptop. Feeling the soreness creep up on me, I grabbed two entrees from a Mexican spot by my condo — one for now and one for later, then hurried home before more side effects kicked in.

A slight headache began to form near my temples as I pulled into the lot. I parked my car and rubbed my head then scoffed before nearly shitting on myself. There he sat on the cemented steps to my apartment.

I considered driving off, but I couldn't take my eyes off of him. The hate I felt for him the past few weeks somehow left my bones. My sight was locked on him, curious as to who gave me up, and secretly happy he was there.

He didn't know I was in the Camry watching him sit with his legs spread apart, and his head bowed down on his suitcase. I stayed put and waited to see his face, suffering through the pulsing aches above my forehead. Moments later, he lifted his head, and I smiled internally. He was still as gorgeous as the day I left him.

He looked in my direction as if he sensed me lurking, then he rose and grinned at me with his dark circles and rugged beard. I didn't smile back. I sat in the car unable to move, unnerved and exultant all at once.

Mash made his way over to the car, and I cranked the engine. Stretching his arms and holding his hands out, he raced to my window. "Please turn the car off," he pleaded.

I kept it running and yelled through the window, "Who told you where to find me?"

He pressed his hands against the glass and stared at me with his sad walnut eyes. "Please. Turn it off and I'll tell you."

I wasn't ready to confront him or hear his incessant apologies, but I did as he asked, refusing to lock eyes with him. Even when I hated him I loved him, so I stared straight ahead, careful not to let his eyes captivate me into submission. My conflicted mind and heart reached to crank the car again. "Please, Nadia," he begged.

Hearing him call my name weakened me. My chest pounded with immense confliction of love, anger, and hurt, but I longed to hear his voice call out to me. So, I refrained. "Get out so I can hold you in my arms," he said.

I looked at him like he was crazy as my neighbor pulled into his parking space beside me. He saw the look on my face and intervened, tapping on the passenger window. "Is this man bothering you?" he asked.

"No, we're fine. Thank you for asking," I replied and curved the side of my mouth.

"Are you sure?"

"Yeah," I explained. "He tells bad jokes."

"I'm her husband," Mash replied. "And you are?"

"Husband? Are you now?" My neighbor questioned. "Is he your husband, 43?"

"Yes. Everything's fine." I nodded.

My neighbor took his slow time walking inside his place, as I took my slow time getting out of the car. Mash squeezed me and felt the enormous bandage wrapped around my arm. I eased away. "What's that for? Are you alright?" He worried.

"It's nothing," I answered.

"You're smaller than I remember. And you look... different. Let me help you."

He grabbed the bags of food from my hands and brought his baggage inside. I waved at my neighbor still spectating, and leaned against the door behind me. Mash stood near the sofa staring at me intensely. "Are you ever going to look at me?" he asked. I looked up and our eyes met. "Do you hate me?" He sighed.

"A little bit," I said, then turned away from him.

"I wasn't expecting you to say yes, but I don't blame you," he admitted.

My eyes returned towards him. "How did you find me?"

He stepped closer to me. "I had help from a few people. My dad was one of them. What's with the bandage?"

I stepped towards the sofa and sat down. "It's good you two are speaking. And this is nothing. My blood dropped, and I had the iron infusion done today."

"Can I hug you?" he asked, hugging me before I could answer him.

"I answered your question, now answer mine. How did you find me?" I fought my hands to hug him back and wandered to the other side of the room.

"Levi."

"I ought to call Taylor and..."

"She didn't tell him. He has tracking on her phone after he found out about— you know."

"Wow. Ha! Good for him. Guess I can turn this back on now." I pulled my cell phone out of my bag.

Mash huffed from across the room. "You don't seem too thrilled to see me."

"Should I be? After the whole spill." I blazed him down with my eyes. "What hotel are you checked into?"

"I was planning on staying here," he spoke with conviction.

"Why?"

Our eyes locked.

"Because I'm your husband. And we have a lot to discuss," he said, hovering over me.

I hummed to myself and leaned my head back on the sofa. "There's a slew of hotels a few blocks from here. I'll drive you over there in a few minutes. Just let me rest for a second," I said.

"Can I get you anything? Is there anything you need me to do?"

"You can tell me why you're really here since you believe I had an affair and put me out of what I thought was our home."

"I want you. I know you didn't..." he paused. "I was out of my mind to think you would ever betray me. I acted out of anger, and you have every right to be pissed at me. But I know you love me. How do I fix what I've done?" He stole a kiss from my forehead.

I didn't respond.

"Can you at least look at me?" He pleaded, rubbing his face against mine. "Nadia. Look at me. I'm sorry. I made a mistake. I'm a fool. The worst person in the world. And I'm miserable without you."

I opened my eyes and looked at him. He meant every word he spoke, but my stubbornness and lack of energy prevented me from jumping into his arms. "Say something," he implored.

"I hear you, but I'm too tired to have this conversation. Can I close my eyes for a few minutes? Please?" I asked, and drifted off before he answered.

When I woke I was covered with one of the blankets the girls left behind on the sofa. Mash sat at the opposite end with my feet in his lap asleep. I watched him for a short while, then closed my eyes again to nap a little longer.

The second time I woke up, it was evening. Mash was awake, reading my medical instructions, warnings, and side effects list from my doctor. "How are you feeling?" he inquired.

"Tired and sore, but I can manage." I removed my feet from his lap.

"Will you tell me if any of these side effects occur?"

"Yeah sure," I answered, shaking my head at his concern.

"This pamphlet says you go back for a reading in a week. What is the reading supposed to tell you?"

"How my body is reacting to the iron. Nothing major," I maneuvered best I could.

"I have some shows coming up, but I'll cancel them so I can go with you."

"No need. It's only a reading." I struggled to stand.

"Let me help you."

"*I got it*. I'm going to take a shower. I don't feel like driving, so I'll bring out some sheets and more blankets. You can have the couch tonight."

He scoffed. "I wasn't going to a hotel anyway," he said.

I rolled my eyes at him and headed upstairs. Mash was on my heels. "Your food is cold, and I didn't see a microwave in the kitchen. I was thinking about ordering a pizza. Do you mind?"

"You have the address. Do as you will." I sighed.

My mind got lost in the shower as my thoughts jumped from one to the next. I had no real recollection of me bathing, yet I was covered in soap with warm water tapping on my back. "Nad, I don't mean to hound you, but you've been in there for a while. Are you okay?" Mash asked.

I snapped out of my daze. "I'm fine. Be out in a second."

I dressed in the spaghetti strap pajama set Taylor bought me and covered in my robe. I removed my satin scarf from my head to dry it from the shower steam and studied myself in the mirror. I didn't recognize the person looking back. *'Thank God I'm getting my hair done in the morning.'* I smirked to myself. *'He thinks he's slick calling me Nad.'*

I curled up on the bed, listening to Mash interact with the delivery guy. The wood on the stairs creaked from his footsteps and he knocked on my bedroom door. "The pizza is here. Do you want a slice, or do you want me to bring your food up here?"

"Is the pizza good?" I mumbled.

"I'm honestly impressed. Wait right here."

He returned with the box and cups of ice, and a two liter of pop. The box sat between us on the bed, and I took a slice and placed it on the inside of the top lid. "This is good," I said. "What made you pick this place?"

"The name. Little Italy. I figured the pie must be good to name their shop after the homeland."

"I'll add this place to my list."

Mash stopped eating. His head dropped and he placed his slice back in the box. "Add to your list? Are you planning on staying here?"

"I signed a twelve-month lease," I said.

"We can break it," he replied.

"It's already paid for."

"Then **sublet** it." He raised his brows.

"And go where? London? To your house?"

"Home. To our house."

I wiped the crust from the sides of my mouth and prepared to be badgered from my response. "I had my own house, and no one could tell me when to come or when to get the fuck out. You reminded me of that. I like being in control of my life and need to have my own shit from here on out. I can't trust..."

"How long am I going to pay for my mistake? We've had weeks to cool off and reset, but you act as if you don't miss our life together."

"I miss us. But look at me. I got sick behind you. I couldn't eat, couldn't sleep, or keep anything down on my stomach. I'm worried about what direction my life is headed in. Not you. You weren't rejected and tossed out like old socks. You didn't have to find somewhere to sleep in the middle of the night, or figure out how to start over. You cut me deep," I explained.

"I know I did." He approached me.

"I will **never** put myself in this position again."

"So you hate me." He dropped to his knees.

"I want to hate you, but I don't. More than anything I want to hurt you the way you hurt me. I can never call your house, home again."

He grabbed my face and kissed me on the lips. I fought the urge to reciprocate. "I love you," he said.

"Love is not enough. Look where love got me." I pulled away.

"It got us here. Together again. You tried to hide from me but I found you. Love keeps bringing us together no matter how many times you run away."

He had a point. I had a good run of hiding from him. I covered my tracks well and he still found me, but he didn't earn any points with me because he showed up at my doorstep. I leaned back on the pillows. "Can we clear the air? Get everything out in the open and address all of our issues."

"I don't need to know anything else," he said. "I know enough and want to move on from this. With my wife."

"And this is why I live here and you live there. It's your way or no way. We can't move on if we're carrying baggage from our pasts." I threw the crust of my slice of pizza in the box.

"Nadia, I reacted erratically because of how that douche was calling your name." His face shriveled. "Images of you with him made me lose my shit."

"I owe you an apology," I admitted. "I'm not one hundred percent innocent in all of this."

Mash's shoulders stood erect, and his face turned a pinkish and reddish hue. He pushed the pizza box out of the way and placed his head at the foot of the bed. "What do you mean?" he mumbled.

"Make sure you listen this time. The night I met Lucas, I was meeting Chili and some of his friends at a bar. He witnessed a weird interaction between Chili and me, and followed me out of the bar to see if I was okay. I told him I was married, and he threw his card in my purse in case I needed anything."

Mash covered his face and asked, "What happened with Chili?"

"Nothing happened, per se." My voice rose. "We're cool, but I did tell him you never liked him."

"And the wanker in New York gave you his card, and you called him?" He grunted.

"I did. One day I asked him for references to check out, and he offered to show me the new development in Brooklyn. I thanked him, but he wanted to keep in touch with me. I refused and wouldn't give him any information about me. So, he gave me that phone to keep me updated about things going on in the city. I mailed it back to the address on his card. The messages you heard *was* me avoiding him."

Mash stared at me with anger and confusion across the top half of his face. "What I'm hearing is you went on a date with him."

"Not a date. A tour. And it was innocent. He knew nothing about me except my name was Nadia. No last name, your name, nothing." I crossed my hands.

"Well, he knows it now. Have you talked to him?"

"No! Why would I?" I frowned.

"Okay. Okay. Sorry I asked. He told me he kissed you."

My heart skipped and my eyes popped wide. "When did you? How? Wait. What? He told you what? When did you speak to him? Why would you speak with him?"

"Your phone was last tracked in New York."

"And you thought I went running to him. Wow." I jumped to my feet and left him in my room.

My face burned from his assumption. My head roared with a headache. "Maybe you should stay at a hotel!" I yelled from the stairs.

"What else was I supposed to think, Nadia?!"

I stormed back up the stairs and threw my new house shoes Khai bought me at him. "Did you realize I was telling the truth before, or after you spoke with him?"

"Before I clocked him a few times." He reenacted what he did by punching the air. "Trust me, he had it coming after how he disrespected you. But he confirmed what I already knew." He smiled.

"My word should have been good enough."

"Terrible mistake on my part. It won't happen again." He

placed his hands on my shoulder. "By chance did he tell you he has three children, whom he abandoned because of a domestic violence charge?"

I shook my head no. "I should have never asked him to show me around. This is all my fault. And for that, I'm sorry."

Mash looked at me with those brooding eyes and grin I found hard to resist. He fidgeted with his phone and placed it on the bed, then reached for my hand pulling me in closer.

My favorite song began to play from his playlist, and he swayed us side to side. I placed my head on his shoulder as Sting belted out the words, "*If he loves you, like I love you.*"

"You're not playing fair." I smiled.

"I know I'm not." He sneered.

"What if I were to say turn it off?"

"You won't."

We chuckled.

He tightly squeezed my lower back, and I reclined in his arms. My sore legs wavered with the tempo, and my arms clutched him firmly. His hands ran up and down my spine, and I wilted further in his grip, nearly collapsing from weakness as everything felt right with the world.

The touch of his lips nibbling on my neck, exhaling deep breaths of exhilaration invoked my hidden arousal. I lifted my head from between his strong pecs, and he caught my lips as if he'd been waiting for them.

I, too, was eager to feel his lips against mine, and joined him in a tender lip lock. "I miss you," he said, moaning in my ear.

I mumbled, "I miss you, too."

"Forgive me, and say you're mine again."

"I need time," I whispered.

"What if we don't have time? Say I'm yours, and you're mine, then tell me I can have you."

I backed away and observed the lust mixed with adoration

in his eyes. My chest pounded with force I could hear in my ears. *'Don't be so easy,'* I thought.

I released his hands and placed mine on my knees. Breathless, I bowed down. "I'm not ready to do this."

"You don't want me anymore?" He teared up.

"I do. But not like this."

I crawled under the covers and turned my back to Mash. He stood over me fuming with his hands on his hips, then closed the box of pizza, and packed up the drinks. "I'm going to hop in the shower and let you relax. If you change your mind, need me, or want anything, I'll be downstairs."

"Good night," I said.

The temperature in the house was perfect, but my fatigued body was burning up. A known side effect. Also, a reaction to my gorgeous houseguest asleep on my couch.

I craved his perfect weapon inside of me, rekindling the fire only his spark could ignite, and make me feel like a woman. But forgiveness was my kryptonite. I struggled to get past him making me feel like a desperate bitch out in the street weeks ago— a real life version of the song by Oran Juice Jones telling the woman to leave with only the things she came with.

The hurt and humiliation he handed me surmounted his words of "I'm sorry." But still I checked the clock every two minutes until an hour had gone by, wanting a piece of him.

I threw the covers to the other side of the bed, desperate for a waft of cool air to breathe over me from the vent. It was quiet downstairs. I assumed Mash was sleeping off the tension and travel.

I tiptoed down the steps, crept into the kitchen, and jumped at his silhouette standing near the window. "You startled me," I gasped.

He was sexier than I remembered. The moonlight illuminated his shaved bare chest with a few hairs attempting to stubble free. I was a sucker for him when he walked around in Bruce Lee mode, barefoot and shirtless in pajama pants. "You couldn't sleep either?" he asked.

"Nope. I can't seem to get comfortable."

"You think it's one of the side effects?"

"Perhaps. You're really concerned about those side effects," I sassed.

"I don't like seeing you ill." He turned towards me.

"I'm okay. It got a little hot upstairs, so I came down to get one of my cubes. What are you doing in here?" I asked, reaching for the tray in the freezer.

"I was hoping you had a beer or something stronger to help me wind down, but this place is damn near hollow. You don't even have crisps. What do you have there?"

"This is a Kool-Aid cube."

"A what?" His face wrinkled.

"We ate these when I was a kid. Grams would make Kool-Aid, which is terrible for you by the way, and pour some into empty ice cube trays. Before they were completely frozen, she would stick toothpicks in them, and we would eat them like mini popsicles. Try one." I held out my hand.

"A second ago you said it's terrible for you. Why are you eating it?"

"Because they're delicious," I answered, humming as I licked it.

His judgmental face switched from wrinkled to humored. "Maybe I will try it," he said, taking the cube from my hand. He held the toothpick upside down and ran it across my lips, causing it to melt a trace along the path he drew. He leaned in and sucked the melted juice. "This is good," he said, "The best thing I have ever tasted."

Gazing into my eyes, he inserted the cube into my mouth briefly, then asked, "Can I have another taste?" I nodded yes, and he kissed me gently, then pulled back. My chest pounded violently as I stared at him. My loins screamed, 'Please take me,' as he traced my neck from east to west with the flavored ice in his mouth.

I held my breath and gasped for air. Reaching for my shoulder, he slid my strap down to my biceps, then traced my nipples with what was left of the flavored ice.

I *peaked* a little in my panties as my breasts saluted his mouth, inviting him to play with them longer. He read my body's needs and cupped them with his tongue, pinching them delicately the way I liked. "Mmm," I moaned, feeling the cut of his abs and dip right below it.

Face to face we stood staring at each other, panting of what was to come. Knowing I yearned for him he said, "Don't deny me," then slowly ran his hands from my cheeks to the back of my hair, tonguing me like ice cream.

My lower back held firmly pressed against the island, and his hands unfastened my pinned hair while his fingers rummaged my scalp. He guided me back with a fistful of my tresses, and licked me from my neck down to my slit.

My shorts fell to my feet along his path, "No panties," he grinned, then pressed his nose against my landscape and sniffed. "Mmm, that's it," he groaned. I looked to the ceiling while the sensation of his tongue ran across my skin then inside to my flesh. I shuddered from the relief his lips gave my pussy, and whined in ultimate reprieve. "I've missed this pussy," he whispered.

"It missed you, too," I hummed.

My thighs grew limp, and my hands played in his hair while he licked and sucked and kissed and flicked and tongue twisted my labia. I trembled in his mouth as his hands clutched my ass towards him, eliminating any space to creep between us.

My body grew weary, relying on his strength to hold me up by my thighs to stabilize me in position.

Finally, he came up for air and inhaled sharply, ending his tongue's caress, and lunged inside my oval house of pleasure. I exhaled a painful squeal mixed with notes of bliss. He exhaled a rigorous grunt of delight, plunging deep into my abyss, "You still love me?" he panted.

"Yes," I whispered.

"Tell me," he demanded, stroking stronger.

"I still love you."

He grunted and grumbled with every stab, sinking his teeth into his bottom lip. I rose up the side of the island from his jabs, shrieking when he lifted my ass to the edge hanging halfway off.

He pointed my legs towards the light fixture above, carving his outline into my walls while kissing my thighs and my calves.

"That's right. Rain on me, baby. I'm sorry I've got you all backed up. Get it all out," he ordered. "Come for me."

I purred and pulsed around his dick, quavering in delight from the much needed maneuvering and stabs delivered to my cave. Without warning, he slanted his cock and pressed tightly inside, exuding unsteadily inside of me. He shook, clutching onto the back of my calves as support while I gripped my pussy around his dick tightly, selfishly wanting him to stay inside my lubed warmth.

I was on the cusp of my second rain, and didn't release my hold of his cock until I spritzed on him once more. Kissing my calves, he moaned quietly, wanting more of me. And I the same. My legs remained elevated atop the linoleum, while he raided the fridge for water.

He placed a plate on my stomach and stacked slices of cold pizza from the box on top. He handed me the bottle of water, and carried me upstairs to the bed with the plate securely in tow on my belly.

Carefully, he laid me on my side of the bed, then climbed over me and the pizza, placing the plate between us. We shared a slice— him feeding me whenever I opened my mouth until we finished off the pie.

We shared the bottle of water, and he held me face forward in his grasp, huddled in silence. Words weren't needed. We spoke with our eyes and watched each other blink until we fell asleep. Me in his arms and my hand in his. Finally, I was at peace.

Chapter 9
Mash

The dark sky was on the verge of turning misty blue. The lack of drapes allowed me the privilege to see her from the light which crept between the shades. My sweet was where she belonged, lying in my arms, sleeping peacefully, and beautiful as ever.

I didn't disturb her as she appeared to need the rest. The agony I felt waiting for her to wake, felt as horrid as not seeing her face these past three weeks. I slid below the sheets and draped her cocoa legs over my shoulders, and woke her with sensuous kisses to her supple folds.

I yearned to taste her, mount her, and feel her. I savored her sweetness on my tongue, readier than ever to put my cock inside her once more and hear her call my name.

Alas, she gasped and woke. We hadn't spoken since she dripped mercilessly on me downstairs— Which was fine for me as her body intertwining with mine was all the talking I needed.

I held her thighs and pressed my mouth against her vertical smile, sampling her pussy first thing in the morning like I did back home. She jittered in my hands, sighing of ecstasy above me. I finished worshipping her and gazed into her glistening sandalwood eyes, hoping she realized how much I needed her.

I brushed my nose against hers. She blushed in my caress, and we locked lips with our desires in sync. Her intoxicating scent powered me. I spun on top of her and pressed my hardness against her thigh. She placed her arms around me, ready to receive my morning wood.

I stared down her nose and swept my hands against her temple, then down past her navel, feeling her wetness slick my fingers. I wanted more of her. I slipped back below the sheets and hard licked her north of her orifice. Pressing my lips against her hot spot with force always got her going, so I rolled my tongue into her hole making her squirm, then made her folds disappear into my mouth. "Maximus!" she screamed.

'That's it, my love. Call me. I'm yours.'

Surprising her in the middle of my service, I gripped her ass and rolled on my back bringing her with me. I didn't need to tell her what to do. She rode her perfect brown ass on my face like a cycle, and I grew harder from the respirations she panted.

Her thighs clenched my cheeks, blinding me. Her tight pussy vibrated on my tongue. I didn't need to see her rubbing her nipples with a light touch in circles. It was a given she was pinching them as she rocked. She always did. "Unh," she belted, warning me she was ready to slide down my dick and rodeo me like a bull until the sun made the darkness disappear.

I loved looking at her fuck me. I loved her. Period. I wondered what she was thinking about while I was inside of her. *'Was she going to forgive me? Was she coming home with me? Did her body ache for me as mine ached for her? Did she know how lost I felt with her gone?'*

The rest of the world ceased to exist when she was fucking me. She moved her hips side to side, then around in a rhythm of her own I never figured out. She drove me crazy, and this time I would last way longer than before.

Whenever distance was between us, I never lasted long. She was the only woman whose touch affected me in such a way— so much to handle, I lived to be inside of her.

I had to look at her. I missed her gorgeous face. The way her tits bounced around when she really got into it, and how she guarded them when she came. Jackpot. Right on cue.

I removed her palms and kissed the curves of her breasts to enhance her climax. I grinded her from below with two deep thrusts then paused against the back of her wall. She gripped the back of my head while she screamed, *"Supaman Luva!"* Man, when she spoke in street talk I damn near lost my mind every time.

I rolled her over and plowed her ass into peril— I was her assailant. After she vibrated on me, I pulled out and went back down on her for a few kind licks, then slid back in for more punishment. She hollered my name, "Maximus!" Good grief she knows how that excites me.

I whispered in her ear, "The one and only Mrs. Sharper," drilling her to bits. I wanted to remind her she was mine, and her gold belonged to me and me only. I stamped my name on her ass and her brain, and I held back my climax by pulling out and rubbing it against her clit— a move she begged for.

"Maximus!" she implored, yearning for me to put it back inside.

I resisted. I paused and tasted her luscious lips until I couldn't resist her warmth anymore, gliding back inside to finish her.

I pounded my baby intensely into the bed. The box spring shifted and the headboard sounded as if it were damaging the sheetrock behind it. Her hands around my neck, and her legs wrapped around my waist, "Ah!" I exerted and trembled inside of her.

"Don't take it out," she commanded.

I happily obliged, lied on top of her, kissed her shoulders, and ran my fingers up and down her face until she drifted off to sleep. I fell to her side and followed her lead, a whole man again, hoping she didn't break my heart when the sun lit the sky.

The alarm on her phone woke us a few hours later.

"Good morning, sweets. Do you have somewhere to be?" I asked, kissing her cheek.

"I have a hair appointment in an hour." She rolled her fists on her thighs.

"Care if I come with?" I removed her hands and rubbed her legs. "Are you feeling alright?"

"My legs feel sore," she answered. "You want to come with me to the salon?"

"Why not? I can treat you to lunch after."

"If you insist." She rolled out of bed.

I followed her inside the brick building, and the hostess escorted me to a waiting area. I had an hour and a half to kill, so I stepped outside for a stroll of the plaza.

The shopping village was quaint with coffee shops, off brand clothing boutiques, bakeries, cafes, and a one of a kind furniture store. I spotted a carved wooden table with jagged edges in the window. *'Nadia would love that,'* I thought.

Inside I inquired about the piece and bought it, unsure of the message I would be sending if it were delivered to her apartment. Fearing she might think I was in agreeance of her living there, I paid a ton for the owner to ship it to our house in London. *'She's gonna freak when she sees this.'*

After an hour of killing time, I made my way back to the salon. The hostess was absent at the front desk. I walked towards the area where Nadia was being serviced, and the room fell silent. "Excuse me. I'd like to have a word with my wife." I cleared my throat with every eye in the room upon me.

"Come here." Nadia signaled.

I kneeled down. "How much is your tab?"

"Ninety dollars," the stylist answered.

I pulled out a one-hundred-dollar bill wrapped with a fifty-dollar bill inside of it. Nadia took them both and handed them to the woman. "She brought me back to life, so she deserves a big tip" she said.

I grinned. "As long as you're smiling."

I made eyes with the stylist and thanked her. "I'll be waiting for you out front." I kissed my wife on the cheek, and returned to the front of the salon.

Moments later, Nadia walked out with her hair flowing and a huge smile, beaming with the confidence I remembered.

I showed her the shops I walked through in the village, and a café I thought we could try. We sipped margaritas while narrowing down our order. "The Mexican food you had yesterday makes me want to try this cilantro hummus," I said.

Nadia chortled and chuckled unlike before. "Say what now?"

"What's so funny?" I questioned.

"Nothing," she answered, tapping the front of her throat and giggling under her breath. "I'm fine."

"Should I order it or not?"

"I don't want any, but please help yourself." She laughed softly.

Sitting across from Nadia glowing and happy, made my world shine. I watched her talk with her mouth full, her almost crooked smile, and her bosoms teasing me with her perfect posture, feeling like the luckiest man in the world. *This is how it should be. Always.*

"Are you happy?" I asked her.

She swallowed the last bit of her meal and answered, "Not really."

"How can I change that?"

"I don't know if you can. I was contemplating seeing a shrink. I need to sort my shit out. Make sense of this predicament. Fix whatever is broken with me," she confessed.

"You're not broken. We've both made mistakes, but I'm ready to move past them. I was hoping you were ready to move on as well."

"I'm not there yet. I do want things to go back to the way they were, but it can't happen with the snap of a finger." She gestured.

"It's been three weeks," I huffed.

"And? I wasn't ready to face you. I wasn't ready to face anyone. I was wallowing in my sadness. Giving myself the time I need to think, feel, cry, scream. The me you saw yesterday was a vast improvement from the weeks prior. I'm not loving myself right now, so how can I love another person?" she explained.

"You don't love yourself?" I reached for her hand.

"I'm a mess. I make terrible decisions, and I would like to be a better person. I struggle with forgiveness immensely, and it weighs me down. I've hated myself these past weeks."

"We have that in common."

She paused and scowled. My admittance of hating myself stopped her rant. She raised her hand forward and finally accepted mine, giving me hope. "I don't want to be with anyone else. I want you. I had you. Then I lost you," she said.

"You never lost me. Come home with me," I begged.

"I told you, I need to be on my own for a while."

"Where, Nadia? Here?" I released her hand.

"Wherever I decide. Here. Charlotte. Maybe London. Maybe anywhere." She looked away from me.

"Most of those options are away from me. What about last night?"

"Last night was mind blowing. It always is, but can you honestly say we're meant to be with the fuck-ups you and I have made?"

'This is a new side to her.'

"Our good outweighs our bad," I said.

"This ordeal made me realize I lost myself in you. I've become dependent on you." Her face scrunched.

"Am I being punished for providing for us? I don't get what you're saying?"

"The house is not mine. I could never afford it, and I was thrown out of it. I'm never going to be comfortable in there."

"We'll sell it and move again. Khai told me what happened to you. If I would have known I wouldn't have said what I said."

"Maybe. Maybe not. My point is I shouldn't have put myself in that position again."

I sighed. My apology was not being accepted. Her forgiveness I'd never receive. I looked at her differently for the first time after our exchange. I was far from the dog house. Nowhere near the yard. And I was afraid I'd never be allowed back in the gate. "Nadia, what's your plan?"

"What was your plan?" She sassed me. "Come down here, throw me some good dick, and have me following you around like a puppy?"

"Throw you some good dick?" I raised my brows and repeated slowly.

'Who the fuck is this person?'

"Sorry for being brash, but it's how we operate."

"No, we coexist. We fight. We make up. We love hard. We

fight some more. We make love. We laugh. We live. We fuck like rabbits and do it over and over again." My voice carried.

A woman sitting at the table next to us looked our way and smirked. I regained my composure and sat quietly while Nadia continued to be ridiculous.

"What happened, happened. I'm working on moving past it, but until you showed up, I've been planning my next chapter in life. Since you've been here, I'm having to rethink everything to your liking. You're trying to control how and when I forgive you, but it's not up to you. It's up to me," she argued.

I apologized again. "I don't mean to be controlling. I want to right my wrong."

She rose from the table and left me with the check. I watched her from the table, standing outside staring into the sky as her hair blew along with the wind. I paid the tab and joined her on the curb. She walked a few steps ahead of me, strutting and turning heads.

A car blew the horn at her, and she stopped and waited for me to catch up, making my heart sing. She stroked my ego while we walked the block. "The women in the salon fancied you," she said. I didn't respond to her flattery. "Did you hear me?" she asked.

"I heard you, and I couldn't care less," I replied.

We went back to her place and occupied different rooms. I stayed on the sofa and searched for a flight home, crying on the inside as she avoided me upstairs doing God knows what.

As time went on, I lost focus on finding a flight. I burst into her room to demand she come home. She was curled on the bed crying. "Nadia love," I called out to her. She put up her hands, motioning me to stay back, and I obeyed.

Watching her suffer from the pain I caused her tore me to pieces. It hurt even more there was nothing I could do or say to make things right. She turned her back to me, but I didn't leave her side. I stood there listening to her cry, wanting to console her, but respected her wishes and left her alone.

In that moment, I came to terms how conflicted she was feeling, and accepted how controlling and how much of an asshole I was still being. The poor little rich kid toying with the affections of the woman he loved more than life.

When she appeared to settle down, I disobeyed her wishes and wrapped my arms around her until she fell asleep. But I didn't follow suit. I stayed awake and held her with one thing on my mind. *'Do whatever she asks of me to win her back.'*

Chapter 10
Nadia

The look on the girls' faces in the salon made me chuckle on the inside. Often when a woman walks into a barbershop, the men stop talking and the room is hit with a sudden silence. When Mash walked inside the salon, the ladies zipped their mouths shut. Their curling wands stopped clicking, and blow dryers turned off.

I inconspicuously skimmed the room to see their reactions when he approached me. Murmurs softly echoed as the stylists stared at him up their noses, clients peeped above their books, and the shampoo girls stationed near the sink listened in on our conversation. I enjoyed that moment.

Mash kneeled down to my eye level to ask what I needed. Something about him looking down at me reminded me of the night we met. How I swooned over him, the same way the ladies in the salon were, but still he only had eyes for me.

When he returned to the front of the shop, my stylist and I whispered and laughed at how thirsty the women were. But I was no fool. She was thirsty, too.

I said some not so nice things at lunch, but I spoke my

truth. I was happy Mash searched high and low and found me, but I masked my excitement because of my pride.

As much as I desired to be in his arms and erase the past few weeks, I couldn't pretend it didn't happen and forget how easily he threw me away like an expired carton of milk. Forgiving him was where my problem lied, and I would in time, but I couldn't rush it, and neither could he.

I dismissed him, but he wouldn't leave. He watched me come unglued until I laid in his persistent arms, and fell asleep in the comfort of them wrapped around me. When I woke, his side of the bed was empty, his bags were gone, and the only trace I had of him being in the house was dirty towels and a note left for me on the kitchen counter.

> *I stole a lot of kisses before I left.*
> *This isn't goodbye. I'm giving you your space.*
> *You know how I feel and where I'll be. I'll*
> *call you in a few days. Take care of yourself.*
> *All My Love,*
> *Mash*

I felt dejected after reading his letter, but also relieved. I was no longer under pressure to make a sudden decision about what I was going to do, or having to include his feelings while sorting out my own.

It was a new day for me, and I didn't want to spend it wallowing in my loneliness. I dressed in one of the outfits the girls bought me, and drove my fresh new look around the city, open to whatever possibility came my way.

I stopped on the side of the road and grabbed a free *Creatives* paper from the bin. From there I selected random places to go and events to attend, such as standing in a long line for free ice cream because it was National Ice Cream Day.

Then I cheered on marathon runners downtown, baked in the sun at a food truck park, and closed the night at a happy hour intended for the work crowd.

The next day I reacquainted myself with the kitchen and stir-fried a home cooked meal, power-walked in my neighborhood, then read the reviews of therapists online.

Seven days later, I found myself in the office of Dr. Jouer, the therapist with the highest recommendation on Doc.com. The reviews mentioned he was attentive and warm, exactly the type of comforting spirit I needed to help me sort out my issues.

His aura was inviting when he welcomed me into his office. I couldn't help but return his smile, and stare at him as he resembled a middle-aged version of Mr. Robinson with early signs of crow's feet, dressed in a maroon cardigan.

In my head I sang, *'Won't You Be My Neighbor'* as he introduced himself. The temperature in his office was perfect. Atlanta was blazing outside and freezing everywhere you went to escape the heat, but Dr. Jouer's office was cool, comfortable, and cozy.

I lied back on the chocolate suede chaise, introduced myself, and jumped right into my song. "Okay here is what you need to know. I'm only in town for a few weeks, so I need quick therapy. Nothing drawn out over time. I'm married, currently separated from my husband. He's kept secrets from me, nothing sexual, and I recently engaged in a non-sexual relationship with another man. I have a good marriage so what I need to know from you is, did I subconsciously engage with this other man as revenge, or were my intentions something deeper? Was I acting out of character because my best friend was secretly sleeping with the man I initially thought I'd marry? Did I do it because I am somehow threatened by my husband's ex? Or did I do it because my curiosity about something new and shiny dangling in my face intrigued me when it shouldn't because I'm crazy about my husband?" I exhaled.

"May I?" Dr. Jouer asked.

"Sorry. I totally took over." I covered my face then pulled my eyes out wide.

"It's nice to meet you, Mrs. Sharper. I'm not familiar with quick therapy. Have you received previous counsel prior to today?"

"Um. Yes. Kind of. It was group therapy."

"I see. I'll need a little more information before I can help you sort out what it is you are seeking advisement for."

I filled in the blanks for the doctor with a rundown of our timeline, the magic we shared, the dilemma with his management, the lie he told me about his father, the secret he kept about his ex-girlfriend.

I told him about Dylan and Taylor, Isla and Evan, and Khai's theory that those instances created insecurities within me and led to a string of bad decision making on my part.

"Is your friend a clinical therapist?" he asked.

"No. She's a loan officer." I perked up.

He scoffed and wrote in his notepad. "How many weeks will you be in town?"

"Maybe a month. Maybe longer?" I alluded, with hope he wouldn't attempt to drag out our sessions for years without resolve.

"You have provided some thorough information, but unfortunately our time is up. Can we meet again on Thursday? Same time?"

"See you then, doc." I clicked my tongue and winked at him. "I don't know why I did that. Sorry."

I left his office doubting I would keep the appointment. A weight had been lifted off of my shoulders as I spewed my troubles out loud to him. Hearing myself say it all in one breath, I realized I didn't want anyone else's opinion on my life. I wanted my own.

I sat in the parking lot and dialed Mash. His voice skipped and cracked when he answered. "Babe? How are you?"

"I saw a shrink today," I blurted, assuming he was shocked to hear from me by the sound of his voice.

"I'm not sure what to say to that?"

"I honestly don't know why I told you." I frowned.

"I don't know much about shrinks, but I'm sure it doesn't work with one visit."

"I know... I don't know. We'll see."

"How are you getting on? Say the word, and I'll hop on a plane."

"Don't you have upcoming shows?" I asked.

"Is that your way of saying no?"

"I didn't say no. How are you?"

"I've been better." He sighed.

"I didn't call to upset you. I called to hear your voice and check in. And finish our conversation from the café."

"Nadia, I'm following your lead."

Mash's voice sounded distant and distracted. I grew worried he was slipping away from me, and wondered if I should cancel the reading of my blood results and fly to London. Possibly revisit Smitty's gym and duke out our demons in the ring. '*Slugging it out worked the last time.*'

By the time I made it home, I convinced myself to call the office for my results and catch the next flight out of the states. As I exited the car, the mail carrier startled me. His bag knocked my sideview mirror. "Sorry, ma'am." He smiled. I nodded. I sped in the heat from my car to my door, as he trailed behind me. "I believe this is yours," he said, handing me a box and certified letter. "Sign here, please."

"I'm sorry. You have the wrong address," I argued.

He pointed to my name on the package, "Are you headed to 43. Last name Sharper?" He poked out his lips.

"That's me." I sighed, and signed with the stylus.

I went inside and opened the letter first as there was no sender information listed. My mood shifted south when I saw the name of the signee. Lucas Fucking Fleming.

Nadia, Nadia, Nadia, (Sharper)
It took a lot of bribery and favors, but I finally found you at
this address. I haven't stopped thinking about
you and would love to see you. Actually, I need to see
you. Here's an open ticket to New York. Seeing your
face walk through my door is all I can think about.
I'll be waiting for the day you show up and put me
out of my misery.
Lucas Fleming

I was convinced the devil was sitting on my shoulder with his foot pressed on my neck and having a laugh at my expense. I wanted to run. Anywhere I couldn't be found, or tracked down, or harassed.

Lucas wasn't going to go away easily. He possessed the stupid, damaging note I wrote, and I could feel he was going to be the end of my marriage. Talking to myself I screamed, "You should have never given him false hope!"

His letter caused me to spiral out of control. I pushed the box aside, uninterested of its contents until it ate away at me in the middle of my shower. I left wet footprints on the carpet as I bounced downstairs in my towel and opened the box. Inside was a stunning handbag, surprisingly my taste, and a hand-written message on a card.

The best for the best.

Blend

All my love,
Maximus

I breathed the heaviest sigh when I read his name, dropped to my knees, and cried happy tears clutching the bag hanging from my arm. I hid my face and snapped a photo, then sent it to Mash with the caption:

The best from the best.
I love you!

He called within seconds. "Why can't I see your face?" He sounded aggravated.

"Didn't want you to see me crying. Your gift was right on time. You have no idea. You sound a lot better than you did when we spoke earlier."

He deflected. "Did my gift upset you? I didn't send it to persuade you. Or make you cry."

"These are happy tears. I love it. I love you."

I managed to survive our call without telling Mash about the letter and the ticket. Talking with him swayed me to keep my appointment with the hematologist, and fly out to London after I had been seen.

My fingers twitched while I observed the other patients in the waiting room. An elderly couple sitting across from me held hands in silence, a baby to my left stared at me until I smiled at him, and the woman at the end of the row beamed as she whispered on the phone. The rosiness in her cheeks matched the cheeks of the baby, who lifted my spirits by simply showing me his toothless gums.

"Sharper!" called the nurse.

Down the ivory hall I followed her, into the lab with my

arms being prepped to be stuck yet again. My veins were a nurse's dream. Ripe, plump, and easy to pierce.

In went the needle, and the extraction began. My dark red blood streamed into two tubes, then a ball of cotton cleared the spot of blood before the bright pink tape sealed the hole. "Follow me," the nurse said.

She led me to a small room with an ugly orange chair, observation table, and portable computer on wheels. My thoughts carried away lying on the white paper, and counting the dots on the tile ceiling. I hardly slept the night before, thanks to my mistake from New York looming somewhere in the wind, and despite having the infusion done, I still felt tired.

I drifted off into a nap, and jumped up when Dr. Oliver walked in. "Nice to see you again, Mrs. Sharper. How are you feeling today?"

"Still a little tired. But I didn't get any sleep last night, so it's nothing a nap won't cure," I answered.

"Painting the town red?" he teased.

"I wish," my voice elevated. "A night on the town could do me some good."

Dr. Oliver pinned the right side of his mouth together, "Well, before you go wild in the streets, be mindful of the heat. And continue to take care of yourself. The infusion was successful. You didn't reach a level 12, but your numbers did increase significantly to 11.5, which is good. Now if I remember correctly, you recently moved here from..."

"London," I said.

"Yes. I knew it was from somewhere pretty far. Your results show an HCG level that indicates you're pregnant. That could explain why you feel tired. There are a few OBGYN offices in this building I can refer you to since I assume you don't have one here in the states."

"Pregnant?" My eyes enlarged. "Are you sure?"

"The numbers say so. Would you like for our office to schedule an appointment with a referral?"

"Can I be seen today?"

"Wait here. I'll have the nurse come back in with that information. Congratulations and we'll speak soon."

The short time I waited for the nurse felt like an eternity. I couldn't believe I heard the word pregnant come from his mouth. *'He must be mistaken.'*

I sat there in disbelief, recalculating the timeline of my last period, wondering how far along I was, and sadly questioned what I was going to do about it.

The nurse returned to the room. "Two floors up, you'll find the Women's Care Center. Dr. McGrath can see you in one hour if you would like the appointment."

I nodded as the words, "I do," spewed from my mouth.

The nurse handed me paperwork to complete for the visit. "I'll let them know you are on your way up. You may not have to wait a full hour," she said. I thanked her and skipped riding the elevator to the office. Instead, I walked the two flights of stairs to kill time, and sat on the steps in a daze talking to myself in my head. *'What am I going to do with a baby? Why now?'*

Time seemed to slow down, but the heat didn't as a sweat bead dripped down my nose. Failing to compose myself, I exited the corridor and entered the Women's Center looking like a deer trapped in headlights.

Impatiently I waited for my name to be announced, studying the pregnant women coming and going. Petite, tall, short, and huge women waddled around and put the fear of God in me. I was raised religious, but strayed away after reading several books with different perspectives about faith and spirituality. Yet the idea of becoming a mother led me back to the path of believing in an instant. *'God, I am afraid.'*

I never truly saw myself as a mother and was never sure if I had a maternal bone in my body. Sure, when I was serious with Dylan I imagined having a family one day, but it was what you do when you think you've found the one. I loved my nephew dearly, and smiled at little babies whenever they passed by, but never have I ever pictured me giving birth— and especially not under circumstances like this.

"Sharper," my name sounded from the double doors. I snapped out of my troubling thoughts and followed the nurse into an ultrasound room. Once I stripped off my shorts, I found myself in stirrups, shivering while I stared at a poster of a monkey with the words "Hang in There" below it.

The lab tech asked me to relax, but I couldn't. My legs shook uncontrollably. She buzzed for an assistant to bring me a heated blanket to calm my nerves, and made small talk to distract me from the intrusion about to follow. The speculum wand entered between my legs and I hysterically burst into laughter. "This shit is not happening to me."

I placed my hands over my face, and the tech asked, "Are you doing okay up there? What I'm doing right now is measuring the fetus. It looks like you are coming up on six weeks. I'm turning the sound on now, and I'm going to move around a little bit. Ah, there it is. That's your baby's heartbeat."

An hour prior I didn't know what I was going to do, then the simple sound of two beats continuously thumping inside of me changed my world. My downward spiral no longer had importance, and a little person I'd never met had complete control of my thoughts. Giving me a new purpose to carry on, and become a better version of myself. He or she had been a part of me for weeks, experiencing the lowest point of my life at the start of theirs, and chose to stick around. I was impressed.

I dressed and met with Dr. McGrath afterwards, nodding along to every word leaving his mouth about vitamins, sono-gram pictures, and the calculation of the first day of my last period. My face confirmed I had no idea what he was talking about. "I'm sure you have questions," he smiled.

"Several. I saw blood the other day after having sex." I blushed.

"A little bleeding is normal after intercourse," he confirmed.

"So I shouldn't have sex?"

"Sex is fine. I wouldn't get too wild though."

"Is everything normal, and will travel be a problem?"

"Your baby's heart rate is strong. Traveling now shouldn't be a problem, but not recommended at the end of your cessation. Take care of yourself and we'll see you in four weeks, but don't hesitate to call if you have any concerns or further questions."

I left the center with every concern and question in the world crossing my mind. *'Is everything going to be okay? Will I be a good mother? Am I ready for this? Why me? Why now? Am I crazy? And how am I going to break this news to Mash?'*

<h1 style="text-align:center">Chapter 11
Lucas</h1>

The delivery confirmation verified Nadia's address. I wasted no time booking a flight out of LaGuardia. I had to make my move while she and her husband were at odds, and convince her to free herself from his strings and explore life with me. After all, my sources risked their careers tracking her and her husband's phones for me. It would be a waste to let their efforts be in vain.

The redeye was steep at the last minute, but seeing Nadia's mocha skin illuminating in the night sky was worth every penny. I checked into a hotel overnight and waited for mid-morning to work my way over to her place.

Along the way, I saw many attractive women with wide hips, long hair, bodacious booties, and non-existent waistlines throughout the city. Turns out Atlanta wasn't the country town I pegged it for. But as tempting as those women were, I held out for the one woman on my mind, Nadia. None of them were as stunning as her, and the way she controlled my thoughts these past months, no other woman would ever be. My only hope is this trip down here goes according to plan and she agrees to run off with me.

I stood outside her door for an hour. No one answered when I knocked, so I waited for her to show. I circled the building to see if a light was on inside her unit, and listened closely for her voice inside. The sound of silence assured the apartment was empty.

The heat was blistering, and my clothes reeked of sweat. This wasn't exactly the presentation I had in mind to woo her into my arms. I planned to surprise her and treat her to an expensive lunch, similar to the one we had on 57th, but not in soiled clothing and smelling like outside.

Then hunger struck me, and I was forced to leave against my wishes. I tucked my card under the door knocker and wrote on the back:

I'm in town. Call me when you get this.
Lucas

The following day I faced the same feat. Still no answer at the door. Still no Nadia. I was convinced I had chased a false lead, and wondered who signed my letter with the airline ticket inside.

It was clear Nadia would never stand before me again, and be a memory I'd forever fantasize in my mind. Being so close to seeing her once more and failing, troubled my soul. '*I need a pick me up.*'

To ease my mind of my plight, I found myself at one of the famous strip clubs in Atlanta. And I must say, not only were the women perfectly embodied angels, but the lemon pepper wings were out of this world.

Though I enjoyed the scenery of beautiful black women jiggling and bouncing before me, I still couldn't get Nadia out of my head. My dick grew hard looking at the naked women sliding down poles like angels, and grinding against other patrons. I couldn't wait for Nadia to be in their position. I would make her pay for making me wait so long to taste her, then make it up to her with the best stroke game north of the Mason Dixon.

I needed sexual relief. I called over the dancer eyeing me the moment I sat down. She strutted over from a few feet away and kept me entertained. "I can take you in the back for a few hundred if you like," she offered.

I grinned at how well she read me. "Lead the way," I said, following her down a dark hall.

We passed an open room of *heauxs* hard at work on a *jon*, then slid in a fluorescent purple room a few doors down. She closed the door behind us and I made myself comfortable in a black leather chair.

She circled me, dragging her fingernails around my shoulders and back. "No need for the teasing," I said. "Just get to it."

She looked at me and smiled. I assumed she either liked taking orders, or was ready to alleviate me of my demons. Leaning over me, she slowly lowered her body and rubbed her hands against my chin and licked my lips. I grabbed her by the neck, "I don't kiss *randoms*," and pulled a rubber from my wallet. '*The nerve of this whore trying to kiss me in my mouth.*' I was wasted in that shithole establishment, but not out of my right mind.

She rested her hands on my knees while I *latexed* my johnson. "Go ahead. You know the job," I said, imagining it was Nadia's full lips slurping up and down my dick. When she finished, I kept the bag on my pipe until I left the lot, and tossed it out of the window on the freeway.

I showered back at the hotel, still unable to get my dream girl out of my mind, and hauled ass to the address hoping she was there this time. "I've seen you lurking around here for a few days now! Get lost or get cuffed!" A woman's voice shouted from above.

"I want no trouble, Miss! I'm looking for the young lady in 43! Pretty brown girl, about five-four in height, gorgeous. Simply gorgeous!"

"You don't look like her type!" She chuckled.

"So you've met the husband!" I replied.

"Who are you, the boyfriend?"

"I wish!"

We shared a distant laugh.

"She left with a suitcase, so you're out of luck. But I'm single!" The neighbor cackled.

"I might have to take you up on that offer!" I joked. "You have a good night!"

"You too, sugar!"

I was flattered by the feisty woman in the window. And grateful she verified I had the right address. My ego was bruised with the news of the husband though. *'He must have intercepted my letter,'* I thought, because I was confident Nadia would have reached out to me.

My fight was far from over as I planned to return and try my hand again. If I was lucky, I'd get the chance to lay one on her joke of a husband and even the score. If not, taking his woman would do.

Chapter 12
Nadia

I promised Mash I would call him when I left the doctor's office, but I didn't. I placed my phone on airplane mode, and went to the mall instead. I walked inside every baby store I crossed, fumbling through clothes and scoping nursery furniture.

I couldn't resist this yellow two-piece set with the matching hat and socks. I contemplated mailing it to Mash as the announcement, but decided against it as I wanted to see the look on his face when he heard the news.

After I window shopped for a few hours, I headed home to have my joy stolen. I trashed Lucas's card and followed my initial instinct to skip town. I raced inside, threw a quick bag together, loaded the car, and drove to my mother's house in South Carolina.

My plate was full. Mash was acting normal, a baby was growing inside of me, and now Lucas was back from hell. The anxiety of it all led me to the side of the interstate before I reached the South Carolina state line where I cried hysterically, and had to wait half an hour before merging back into traffic.

I screamed to the top of my lungs while simultaneously singing along with the music blasting, unsure if my outbursts were signs of another breakdown, or pregnancy hormones.

I arrived at my mother's house puffy faced, snot nosed, and red eyed, but as always, her arms eased my pain. My surprise brought a smile to her face briefly. "What brought you to tears?" she asked.

"Nothing," I lied.

"Um huh," she moaned.

She led me to the kitchen and began cooking. "Call your brother and tell him you're here." I did as I was told and cleaned myself up before he and his clan arrived.

We caught up for old times sake, ate until our bellies were full, and I hid everything about my personal affairs.

In the morning, Mom and I drove to see Grams. Three generations with a fourth on the way. We spent the evening dining at a white table-clothed eatery, and on Sunday morning attended church service.

I envisioned the door bursting into flames when my foot crossed the threshold of the Baptist halls. I checked the time on my phone countless times during the sermon until a peaceful spirit surrounded me. *'Grams must have said a silent prayer to ease my anxiety and be present in the moment.'*

After church, the three of us enjoyed what was left of the hot sun on the beach. "What's going on with my gal?" Grams asked.

"Nothing," I lied.

"You lie bad like your daddy." Grams scoffed.

"I thought if anyone could get the truth out of her, it would be you, Mama," my mother added. "She gave me the same answer."

"Nothing's going on," I emphasized.

"Umph, umph, umph. Never thought you'd shut me out gal. It must be something big." Grams stared at me.

"I'm working something out, but when I know for sure I'll tell you two everything. I don't want you to worry if there is no need to worry. That's all I can say right now." They both stared at me until I shouted, "The sun is about to set!"

We quieted down and ended the evening under the umbrellas enjoying the breeze, opposite the sun sinking into the water, and said goodbye.

I waited until Tuesday to return to Atlanta, under the assumption Lucas would have returned back to work. My neighbor called me from her window. "Hey 43, a handsome young man was camped out here looking for you some days ago," she said.

"Are you sure he was here for me?" I asked.

"He didn't call you by name, but he described you to a tee. You in some kind of trouble?"

"No. Why do you ask?" I sassed.

"I don't know many husbands who would like another man staking out his wife's place."

"How do you know I'm married?"

"People talk."

"Thanks for telling me," I said aloud, then mumbled to myself, "I bet she knows everybody's business."

The news of Lucas still lurking around worried me. I had spoken with Mash briefly over my long weekend, and didn't like how he sounded. It seemed only right to share what the neighbor told me— run to him even. But I couldn't resist making him sweat a little and teach him a lesson about not getting what he wanted when he wanted it.

I needed to be firm and prove I could stand strong on my own, so I put off calling him and tackled the dirty laundry from my trip instead. While sorting my load, Gemma, Mash's assistant, popped up on my screen. Chills ran down my spine when I answered.

"Sorry to bother you at this hour. I wouldn't call if it wasn't important," she said.

"You're fine. Is everything okay?" My voice cracked.

"I'm out of line and overstepping right now, but I wanted to mention something to you and hope this conversation can remain between us."

"Okay..." My words dragged.

"Mash has the team concerned. They don't know I'm calling you, but I thought you should know his behavior has been questionable lately. He's been

flying pretty high if you know what I mean."

"Does anyone else know he's...?" I questioned.

"If they do, they won't say. I normally wouldn't either. I'm crossing the line here." Gemma's voice lowered.

"I won't mention this, and thanks for calling. Can you send me his schedule, please?"

"Done. We're in Manchester Arena this weekend. I'll have a car and pass ready for you."

The doorbell rang, and I jumped. "Thanks, Gemma," I whispered, then eased over to the window. A sigh of relief escaped my lips, and I opened the door for the parcel delivery guy.

"Sign here, please." He held out his stylus pen.

Quickly I signed for the package and double locked my door. *I can't live in fear like this,* I thought to myself.

I placed the box on the sofa. I was crossed between sadness of the news about Mash, and annoyed at whatever guilt gift he sent to apologize for using again. I never saw him as an addict, but the picture he painted of those days were vivid enough, I didn't want to experience that side of him. The smoking weed I could handle, but heavy narcotics was a road he would travel alone.

The more I replayed Gemma's words in my head, the more I felt he relapsed because of me. My mind was frazzled, my heart ached, and peace seemed like a dream to never come.

It was clear I was needed in London, so off I went, running to help the man I swore to teach a lesson and make suffer, only to falter when he needed me.

***

Mash was already in Manchester by the time my flight arrived. The car Gemma arranged for my pickup drove me to the house I vowed I would never step foot in again. I took a deep breath, went inside, and checked out every room to kill time.

They were exactly as I left them except for the dishes in the sink, the crumbs on the counter, and my closet. Mash cleaned the mess I left behind. He hung up the clothes I'd thrown to the floor during my rage-fest, restacked my shoes in the squares, hung my bags on the shelves, and placed my jewelry and scarves back on the prongs. *'He truly was waiting on me to come home.'*

I walked to the other end of the house and entered his studio. It was a war zone compared to the other rooms. Completely wrecked. I had never seen it in such a disarray. Wires unsecured, records outside of the covers, microphones lying around out of their sockets, and pizza boxes smelling of old cheese left behind on the pool table next to the residue of a trace of cocaine.

I didn't dare touch his tracks. I left it as is, questioning if I made the right choice to come back and deal with him, and this situation I knew nothing about.

I had more than him to think about now, and I was unsure

if I should check into a hotel and never let him know I had returned, or stay and do what Gemma asked of me.

I double backed upstairs and tripped on my steps when I passed the dining room. It was the one room we hadn't decorated because we couldn't decide if it should be formal, or furnished to Mash's signature style—with a pool table in the middle of it.

A big red ribbon caught the corner of my eye, causing me to misstep. I caught my balance with the wall and entered the once empty space, now furnished with a beautifully hand-crafted maple wooden table.

The edges were cut with a precisive curve, and captivated me with its uniqueness and beauty. It ornamented the room to perfection and felt to be made with me in mind. *'Nice play.'*

Caught up in its details and artistry, my mind temporarily eased in the moment. Filled with forgiveness and hope, I decided I would stay and ran to the store before the car picked me up for the show.

I organized my few ingredients to cook breakfast in the morning. *'Red velvet waffles are a good way to start over,'* I thought, then prettied myself up.

My heart skipped a beat when I entered the coliseum below deck. Gemma met me at the side door with my pass, and handed me off to security who escorted me through a horde of drunks, druggies, and *heauxs* to Mash's dressing room.

When I entered, I knew I made the right choice by staying. Our for better and for worse was being tested, and it was my turn to take care of him, the way he had taken care of me.

Chapter 13
Mash

I needed a good hour to myself before the show started. I hadn't felt like mixing lately, which threw me off of my game. My personal life never interfered with my money in the past, but Nadia and this itch had my world spinning upside down in a pool of descent.

The door opened to my dressing room. "I said don't let anyone in." I fanned my hand.

Footsteps approached closer.

"Even me?"

Her voice raised the hairs on my forearm.

"You showed up quick this time. You must know how bad I need you right now," I confessed.

"What the hell are you talking about?" she asked, then ran her hands across my beard.

"Damn, you feel real this time."

"What are you on? And how long have you been off the wagon?" she questioned me, now running her hands through my hair.

"You normally don't talk to me," I replied.

"Say what?" Her country twang spilled.

"Last time you gave me your look of disappointment when you appeared, but you've never spoken before. What's with the questions?" I asked.

She sat down in my lap, reached for my face, and turned it upward to look at hers. She took her fingers and wiped the residue from my nose. "How long, Mash?" she asked.

"I'm tripping hard," I said.

"Snap out of it. It's me. I'm here." Her hands squeezed my face.

Staring into her eyes I exhaled, "Thank God. I thought I was on top."

"I'm not sure what that means, but I think I get it," she said.

I hugged her waist and sniffed the gardenia in her perfume. "We bought that in Paris, didn't we?" I hid my face in her bosom.

"You have to pull yourself together. You can't go out there like this," she whispered.

I rolled my brows against her bosom. "I have thirty minutes until my set. Does this mean you're back for good?"

"Sort of. I have a few appointments I need to keep. You should come back with me."

"I've never needed you more than I do right now." I kissed her hands.

"Why'd you fall off?" Her face scowled. "Never mind that. We can fix this. Let's make it through tonight and start from there. We'll go home, relax, maybe swim a bit, then have a conversation."

"Have you fallen out of love with me?" I asked.

She flashed her pretty smile and kissed my lips. "Baby, Cupid's arrow is so far up my ass you needn't worry about that ever happening."

I smiled back at her. "You say the wildest things at times."

The stage hand knocked, and Nadia gave me a once over. She planted a big one on me then sent me on my way to handle my business. I put on one hell of a show knowing she was there, and counted down the minutes to get her home and play house.

To my surprise, Nadia wasn't as eager to let me make love to her. Normally we would have left our mark in the dressing room, or jumped bones on the side of the road, but she was hesitant coming to bed.

She cooked and cleaned at three o'clock in the morning. Obviously avoiding me. I offered, "Do you need me to rub you down? Help you unwind from the trip?" She shook her head no and stretched for a bowl up high in the cabinets. I stepped behind her, slid my hands underneath her silk gown and ran my chin against her shoulders. "Do you need some help?"

"I know how you want to help," she answered in a coy manner. "I'm almost done prepping."

"You're driving me crazy in this thing you're wearing. Let's go to bed. Leave this. I'll take you wherever you want to go for breakfast," I begged.

"I promise I'll be done in a sec."

"You're stalling. What is it? The time zone? Whatever it is, we can talk about it." I pressed against her back.

"Not right now." She slid away.

"I can tell you're uneasy. Is it me? Is it the house?"

"Mostly," she answered.

"Isn't what I sent you enough to make everything alright again?"

"A handbag?"

"No. The second package with those Kendall Miles boots you wanted that were sold out."

"I haven't opened it yet. And why would boots make everything alright again?" She huffed.

"I put something else inside the shoe box. Since you have

no clue what I'm talking about, what made you come home?"

"Your voice didn't sound right on the phone."

I pressed my palms on her shoulders and applied pressure to help her relax. "You do still love me." I smiled. Massaging my fingertips against her bones she moaned, "Mmm."

"Allow me to release this tension," I crooned.

"You were really high tonight." Her words cut me.

"You've seen me high before."

"Not to the point of hallucination. I saw what you left in the studio. How often are you doing it?"

"Maybe once a day. Here and there."

"So, what I walked in on tonight..."

"Won't happen again," I promised.

She was pissed, and I didn't blame her. I needed to prove I wasn't an addict, but I wasn't ready to quit. My stash was stocked for at least a month, but she was the drug I needed right then. I could control my use while she was home, and I needed her to curb my appetite.

I followed her every step toward the bedroom. The aroma of her perfume dragged alongside me as we passed the dining room. She paused. "Where did you find this masterpiece?"

"I have been waiting to have this conversation. I saw it in a store when you were at the salon. I knew you would love it so I had it shipped here."

"Damn. You did all of that for me? Thank you." She looked surprised and I didn't know why. "So where do you want to put the other pool table?"

"Wherever you tell me to put it. Now about this table. I think it wants to be broken in," I said, stroking her back.

I pulled her in close and she buried her head into my chest. "Mash, I don't know," she whined and shied away. "I've never been with you like this."

"Like what?" I asked.

"High on lines."

"I'm not high right now. This is me, baby. Say you want me." I nibbled on her face.

"Mash, I..."

She didn't say she wanted me, but she didn't stop me either. I strolled my hands up and down, tracing the line down to the small of her back. She was the missing link to making me feel whole again, and I had to have her to feel complete.

I caressed her gently this time and told her I needed her. She knew I did. I could tell she was aware of how bad her withdrawal was shattering me. "Do you want me, Nadia?" I had to hear her say it.

"I always want you."

"Do you touch yourself thinking of me?" I asked, putting my finger on her g-spot, making her wiggle in my arms.

"Every night."

"See how I know your body so well," I said, now sliding my fingers inside real slow.

"Promise to be gentle," she said, worming about.

"Did I hurt you last time?" I asked, pausing my finger play.

"No. It's been a while since you've slow-whined me." She whirred and wiggled, trying to make me move my fingers.

She was ready.

"Did I make you feel good last time?" I squeezed her labia in between my two fingers.

"I can't think of a time you haven't." She gripped my shoulders.

I loosened my grip, and rubbed her outer layer, not too soft, not too rough. She tightened her thighs when my palms kneaded them. "I'll do you however you want tonight. You want slow, you got it." I bit her bottom lip and tapped on her southern set below.

"Make love to me," she begged.

My fingers left her tunnel and moved back to her g-spot. I thumped it the way she liked me to, stroked it slow, then swiped her clit from side to side. She held on to me and exhaled to Heaven until those lips of hers barely parted, and she grabbed onto her breasts.

"That's one," I said.

"Your turn." She sighed, and pulled for me to slide inside of her.

"Do the thing I taught you," I said, making her wait for me.

"Brace yourself, cowboy."

I steadied myself. My early morning wood stiffened harder than the table I leaned against. When Nadia fulfilled my requests, the magic was inconceivable. Without a fuss, she dropped to the floor and licked her lips. "Is this what you want?"

I jolted in my stance. "It's what I need."

Her swift licks caused me to quiver. I could feel my cock extend further down her throat. She slid it halfway out and played with the tip in between the front of her teeth, and inside the top of her upper lip. I nearly oozed before we fucked.

I slowed her down, painfully retracting my spear from her mouth. "Did I do it wrong?" she asked.

"God no," I breathed out. "I'm trying to hold back. Trust me, I don't want you to stop." I confessed.

She took control and went back in full throttle. Stroking my cock with the inside of her jawline, hard and tight. I called out to the heavens, knowing I wouldn't last a minute if I didn't stop her.

I jerked back and took my shirt off, then covered the chair with it. She placed me back inside and tickled her throat with my pipe and no gag. I retrieved. "Get on top and show me how much you've missed me."

"I thought I did a second ago," she grinned.

"Ooh, you know I like when you talk shit to me."

"You owe me," she said, throwing her leg across my thighs.

My sweets craved me and slid down on my dick nice and slow, then stopped once she got it all in and took a breath. '*She remembered*.' She squeezed her walls around my wood like a long time no see hug, and damn did *we* feel the welcome.

She told me to be gentle, but didn't follow her own request, riding me like an old western flick. I was her horse and she was an outlaw hunted for murder finding justice for her magic carpet ride.

Snug and firm, she gripped my wood. Every now and then she threw her head back, but she always ended up looking back at me. Gripping my shoulders like a headboard, rolling her soft ass on my thighs. She rocked me so hard I thought we were going to break the brand new chair. I could hear the wood roll and the legs creek against the floor, surely scratching it as the chair grazed with her moves. Then she quickly turned and gave me a back shot. I was about to lose it.

I had to hold out a little longer, so I stood up in her pussy while untying the red ribbon from the center of the table. Pressed against the back of her tunnel, I held her in place feeling the gyration of her flesh for a few seconds, then I pulled out. I laid her on the floor and tied her hands to the leg of the table. She watched me in wonder yet intrigue.

Once I had her in bondage, I kissed her body from north to south, then back north to taste her chocolate entrance. She squirmed as she couldn't do anything but take the tickles my tongue slowly delivered.

I wondered why I had never done this to her before as she begged me to finish her, and I was going to, but not before I flipped her over and planted my full face in between her ass.

I took my time and traced her perfect round cheeks with my palms as she crawled to her knees, then I went in for the finale with one deep stroke followed by three more to the left wall, and another curved jab to the right. "Mash," she whimpered below me. I poked and scraped for as long as I could hold out then she screamed, "Maximus!" And it was over.

"Yes, Sweets!" I echoed in return, pressing her skin closely against mine.

"Hold me," she said.

I fell to the floor and untied the ribbon from her wrists. She placed her head upon my chest, and I wrapped my arms around her, kissing her forehead and sweeping her hair. "You're a *gotdamn* animal," she whispered out of breath. "But I loved every minute of it."

Whenever she praised me, I felt like a king, and though I was far from it, the way she stroked my ego was all a man could ask for.

In the morning, I asked Prano to come over and take my stash off my hands. With Nadia showing signs she was coming back to me, I didn't want to take a chance and ruin it. I needed to go cold turkey, and avoid the temptation of sneaking in a toke with her in the house.

He took the package, and Nadia accompanied me to my show, followed by doing what was normal for us. Getting one in, in the back of the truck.

She finally cooked the meal she had been preparing, and on Monday she broke free of me for a few hours. I had the urge to toot while she was out, and there I realized I was an addict. I sparked a joint to kill the impulse, but in addict fashion I compiled the residue she found in my studio and inhaled.

The smell of my joint masked my other high, and Nadia had no idea I betrayed her trust. I hated myself for what I had done. It triggered me to want more. And when Tuesday rolled around, I stupidly let her leave without me, and found myself back on the prowl and yearning for more white.

Chapter 14
Nadia

My time in London was coming to an end, but I managed to squeeze in a lunch date with Olive before my departure. I looked like shit the last time she saw me, so I spruced up for our outing, and dressed in some of the higher end pieces I left behind to compete with whatever fashion trend she was going to arrive in. Denim leggings, ankle boots, a white fitted tank, and a cropped khaki jacket layered me fashionably.

She hailed me when I arrived with her signature sultry smile. "Kiss kiss," she said, air kissing my cheeks before we sat down.

"Did you miss me?" I asked.

"I was worried about you more than anything. Why didn't you call me?" She gave me a stern eye.

"Trust me when I say, you didn't want to be bothered with me these past few weeks. I was a total mess, and went into hiding from everyone."

"Not cool, Nadia. I almost didn't show today. I was pissed you didn't call when you said you would." Her eyes rolled.

"I apologize. Forgive me?" I looked up at her like a chastised child.

"Of course." She tapped my hands resting on top of the table. "You seem to be bouncing back to normal. Good for you."

"It's all a façade. I'm a work in progress, but I'm getting there. Last time was all about me. What's been going on with you?" I hunched my shoulders and placed my elbows on the table.

"Where do I begin?" Her brows raised. "Yohan is slipping. He left his phone unlocked one night, and as soon as I went to pick it up he barged in and locked it."

"What did you say?"

"Nothing. I told you I'm riding this out. I figured it was time I level the playing field."

"Noooo." My tongue dragged.

"Yes," Olive smirked. "Let's just say there is truth to the grey sweatpants rumor. If this guy was half as rich as Yogi I would marry him instead."

"Olive, you have your own money. Why does your partner need to be rich?" I asked.

Olive chuckled under her breath and shook her head. She found amusement in teaching me rich girl codes to live by. "I realized a long time ago, I'm a person who always wants more. Yohan provides me luxury. Sweatpants can't."

"So... does he know he's your dirty little secret?"

"I think he's turned on by it."

"Careful. He might catch feelings." I pursed my lips from experience.

"True. I'll have to make sure he remembers it's strictly physical. I tell you. I don't know how men do it. It's a lot of work lying, hiding, and showering, and pretending. And Yogi has at least two, maybe three he's juggling."

"How do you know?"

"I cracked his code. Listen to the names he calls them. Thick Thighs, Blue Moon, and RT3."

"What's my name?" I questioned.

"Worker Bee," she snickered.

"And yours?"

"Second Wifey."

"Ouch," I mouthed.

"Exactly."

"I do need to reach out to Han for work. Once I decide where I'm going to live," I added.

"You're here. I assumed you two worked things out."

"Not officially. I don't feel comfortable in the house. I'm being a brat I know, but I can't help it."

"Oh, I get it. Now you know why I still have my place here, the cottage in France, and the apartment in New York." She sipped her tea and twirled her eyes.

"Speaking of New York. Lucas tracked me down in Atlanta. He left his card on my door."

Olive placed her glass of tea on the table and stared at me. "How?" Her face wrinkled.

"I don't know. I haven't spoken to him. He even sent a plane ticket begging me to come see him."

"He sounds so basic. I hope you were telling the truth about not sleeping with him." Her chest fluttered as the disappointment rolled off of her tongue.

"I didn't sleep with him. I'm regretting the whole ordeal. Don't get me wrong. He was charming, but nothing special."

"So what did you do with the ticket?"

"I upgraded it to come here."

"Good girl." She clapped her hands. "How does Mash feel about him stalking your place?"

"I haven't told him yet. I couldn't. He went to his job and assaulted him."

"Shut up!" Olive exclaimed in a whisper and enlarged eyes.

"I know right," I muttered. "The whole exchange surprises me."

"Two grown men brawling over you." Olive twisted her lips with a smile. "Very Victorian. I love it."

"I'm told Mash did all the punching."

"Now come on. You have to admit Mash deserves a second chance."

I roamed the café and caught my breath. "What would you do if Yohan told you to get out?" I asked her.

She moaned with an exhale. "*Yeesh*, I don't know. I would definitely leave, but I can't say if I would go back to him or not. But Mash isn't Yohan. He's going around beating up guys for you. He made a mistake. I doubt he will ever make it again. And if you could have seen how he stormed into Yogi's office, you would know how passionate he is for you. You'll do what's right and move back here and be my bestie."

I left our lunch date swayed in the direction of moving back for good. I returned to the house and smelled the *loud* before fully coming in from the garage. But I didn't complain. I was excited I had reached a decision, and was in the mood to confess all of my secrets and make a fresh start.

I tested the waters slowly. I told him I was coming home, and asked him to come back with me a second time. He considered it, but didn't give me a definite answer. Then I eased in the hard part. "Lucas sent me a letter and left his card on my door at the apartment."

Mash punched a hole in the wall and lashed out at me for not telling him sooner. "I can't go back with you, so you need to cancel whatever it is you have scheduled and stay home," he demanded.

"What I have scheduled is important. I can't," I explained.

"I'm not letting you go back without me."

"Letting me?" I questioned.

"What if he does something to you? I'm all the way over here. I'm telling you, he is a dodgy fella that one."

"I'll go to my appointments then stay with my mother, or in Charlotte with the girls until I've settled my affairs. Plus, the group trip to Miami is coming up. We can meet up there."

"You're staying here, and we'll both have to miss the trip," he said with his chest.

"I gave Shannon my word we would be there."

Mash paced around the studio, now clean and in order from when I arrived. His blood moon colored eyes looked at me. "I warned your little boy toy to stay away. I'm going to have to..."

I cut him off, "Do nothing. And don't you ever call him my boy toy again."

Our conversation died briefly, and I pointed to him. "This is exactly why I didn't want to tell you."

"I don't trust him." He gritted his teeth.

"Neither do I. But if you're so worried, come with me. I promise I'll make it worth your while," I hinted.

"I can't."

We were at an impasse. He wouldn't reveal why he couldn't come with me, and I didn't reveal I wanted him to be present for the next pregnancy appointment.

Mash saw me off for the airport. I couldn't shake the feeling that what he couldn't discuss with me, had something to do with his sobriety, or missed contractual engagements due to his habit. His secrecy occupied me as the driver maneuvered through the thick traffic until we were stuck.

Barely moving gave me time to think about my choice to return to the states alone. Mash's concern caused me to suddenly fear Lucas's passion for me. The desperation in his letter led me to wonder, '*Could he hurt me and the baby for rejecting him?*'

Impatient with the traffic and a sudden change of heart I asked the driver to take me back to the house. He rode the median to the next exit, and returned me where I belonged. I used my key to the front door and ran inside of the house, bursting through the studio door where I knew I would find Mash. "I don't want to be without you another minute," I said.

"Nadia, it's not what it looks like," he stuttered.

"It looks like you couldn't wait for me to leave."

"This was the last of it. I swear. I can't go back with you because I'm going to rehab. I sign in tomorrow. Please don't look at me like that," he begged.

"I don't know you!" I cried. "I won't be hitched to a junkie."

His face sank and his chest pounded intensely through his shirt. "A junkie? I'm not on the street begging people for money. I'm in the privacy of my home." His voice trembled.

"You've got a little something on your nose," I said and slammed the door.

I ran back to the car and ordered the driver to get me to my flight by any means. I replayed Mash's rehab confession over and over in my head as I boarded the plane, but the image of him sniffing made him unattractive in my eyes. And leaving him behind on the verge of tears hurt like hell, but I meant what I said. I **could not** and **would not** be attached to a junkie.

Chapter 15
Nadia

My world was in *The Upside Down*, and though I left the man I vowed to love for better or for worse thousands of miles away, he was still with me when I arrived back in the states.

His gift sat on the coffee table staring at me when I walked through the door of my condo, taunting me before I could settle in. It haunted me for two days after ignoring it and him, until I made the mistake of listening to his sad voicemails.

Hearing the grief and stress in his voice broke me. He was suffering, as was I, and avoiding his calls accomplished nothing. I felt his pain through the phone and could no longer be mad at him, when I realized what I feared the most was his disease.

Overcome with compassion and clarity, I stopped pretending I didn't care and answered the next time he called. "You worry the hell out of me," he said when I picked up.

"I apologize for not taking your call. I needed some time to process things."

"Call me selfish, but I need to know you are okay? Are you

being careful? And aware of your surroundings?" His voice dragged.

"I am. I shouldn't have left you like that. I want you to know you aren't in this fight alone."

"You might love me after all. I thought I would have heard from you once you opened the box."

"It's still sitting on the table," I mumbled.

"Please, open it while I'm on the phone." He insisted.

Inside were the stunning boots I fancied over for months, along with a copy of the deed to the house, solely in my name. I held my breath as he called my name on the line. "It's yours. All yours. I'm a tenant living in your house," he joked.

"I've seen the bank statements. Nothing reflects a purchase this big."

"Stop playing detective. You said you wanted to be a home-owner— Have security. Now you have it. If anyone has to leave it'll be me."

"I'm coming home."

"I won't be out of here for a few weeks. I want to get well for you."

"Don't do it for me."

"I do everything for you."

"I know."

———

I began organizing the little I had in my apartment after our call. Still terrified of the unknown territory of addiction, but excited to finally be on the same page again.

For a second I contemplated leaving everything behind, flying back to London, and skipping the weekend with the gang. While wrestling with my decision, I ordered a pizza from the place Mash discovered, and called Khai to share the latest. She was rooting for us after all.

We agreed to sign the car over to my brother, keep the apartment as a weekend getaway for the group until the lease expired, and discussed how to divvy up the furniture when that day arrived. She convinced me to stay and allow Mash to do the work in the clinic. "You being so close by is only going to make him want to sign himself out early," she said. "I'll rally the group, and we can make it a party weekend in The A. Sit tight. We'll come down and keep you company."

"The couch isn't going to be enough. I'll pick up another floor mattress later on tonight," I added. "Hold on, my pizza is here."

I went upstairs to grab cash for a tip and looked out of the window before opening the door. "You cannot be here!" I shouted.

"Who are you *shouting at*?" Khai asked.

"Lucas is at the door," I whispered.

"I have to talk to you, Nadia!" He exclaimed.

"I don't want any trouble. Please, just leave," I begged.

"Are you alone?" he asked.

"Say no." Khai whispered on the phone as if Lucas could hear her.

"No. Jesus, Lucas. Get a clue. I haven't spoken to you in months. What do you want?"

"You." He sighed.

"Not going to happen. Now please leave."

"Is he telling you what to say? This doesn't sound like the girl I remember. It sounds like the flake who came to see me to size up his competition."

"You might have to call the police, girl," said Khai, still whispering.

"Did your soon to be ex-husband tell you he sucker punched me? I owe him one. Tell him to come out here and fight me. Winner gets you. Go ahead and kiss him goodbye. I didn't come here to lose."

"Lucas, go home, okay?"

"Do you know how long I've waited to hear you call my name?" He placed his palm against the door. "At least let me see you."

"I'm not opening this door." My brows raised.

"Then come to the window." His voice seductively lowered.

"No."

"Then I'm not leaving. But it's cool. I'll wait out here. Go ahead and pack a bag. You already have a ticket to fly out of here with me."

"I'll mail you a check for it. What do I owe you?"

"I don't take money from women. I'm a man, sweetheart."

My palms grew sweaty, and my chest pounded with pain. Nerves filled my stomach as I fought the urge to hurl. "I owe you an apology," I confessed. "I made a mistake and was wrong to get entangled with you. My note sent the wrong message. Do you still have it?"

"Let me see you, and I'll answer your question."

He must have heard the desperation in my voice, or sensed the fear flowing in my veins of the damage he could cause if he showed Mash my words when I bid him farewell.

I went to the window and let him see me through the screen while Khai continued to listen through the speaker. "Damn I wish you'd let me have you. Do you know how many nights I've dreamed about this moment? I can make you happy and forget about this clown you call a husband. He must not be home, or he would have come outside by now," he baited me.

"Do you still have my note?" I raised my voice.

"Not anymore. I burned it. I got upset you hadn't called and *swish*, I lit it in flames." He gestured an implosion with his fingers. "Why won't you admit you felt something for me?"

"I liked you, Lucas. As a friend. But nothing more."

"Bullshit. You saw we had chemistry, got scared, and cut me off."

He wasn't lying. *'But I was also being stupid and reckless in New York without knowing anything about this man.'*

"I thought you wanted to be my friend. Until you didn't. I made it clear I love my husband. You took advantage of my loneliness, and I almost fell for it."

"You can love two people, Nadia, and I think you do. If I have to share you with him, I will."

"Khai, this motherfucker is crazy," I whispered into the phone.

"Do I? Have to share you?" His voice shook.

"Why did you tell him we kissed?"

"He rubbed me the wrong way. I said it to get under his skin at the time, and it worked. You could have done better than him." He gloated and tugged on his beard.

"goodbye, Lucas."

"I'm not leaving."

"Okay. That's enough. You tried. He isn't responding to you being nice. Call the police, Nadia!" Khai yelled through the phone.

"I'm dialing 911 now," I said.

"Wouldn't be the first time I've been to jail. I'll go for you." He smirked.

"Fine. Sit out there and wait on them to cuff you. I'm done with this," I said, lowering the shades.

I walked away and he yelled loud enough for my neighbors to listen in. "Have dinner with me, and I'll leave! I promise. Have dinner with me tonight."

"I told you I'm not alone. I can't do that." I lied.

"Tomorrow night then. My hotel."

"Hell no." I laughed.

"You pick the place then."

"City Kitchen in midtown. Look it up. Nine o'clock. And no funny stuff."

"Tomorrow night it is." He smiled with hands in a praying pose, then walked off to his car with his chest poking out.

Khai scolded me as I wrote down the make and model of the car he was driving. "Have you lost your mind?!" She lashed out at me.

"Not completely," I replied.

"Why did you agree to meet up with him?"

"To get rid of him."

"And if he comes back?"

"I won't be here. I'm packing up now and getting the hell out of here. Tonight."

"Thank God!"

"I'll be at my folks'. Guess you all will have this place to yourselves for the weekend. I'll call you from the road after I've run a few things by Levi."

Chapter 16
Mash

Hearing Nadia call me a junkie felt like a slap to the face. I wasn't blowing near as much as blow as I used to. Then I heard myself. I sounded like an addict. And snorting the residue off the table was my wake up call.

When she left, I could tell she was done with me. The hatred and redness in her eyes I felt to my core. She was calm in her words, but her face couldn't disguise the disgust and contempt she felt for me in that moment. Her lack of emotion almost neared repulsion, and when she didn't answer my calls, I knew I fucked up. The silence was loud and I heard her.

The challenge of rehab was difficult without Nadia's support. My one phone call a day went unanswered for days, and having no communication with her made my nostrils itch. I was on the brink of checking myself out early to go find her, then she finally took my call.

Her forgiveness gave me hope I could beat my demon. She was returning to me, and knowing she was coming home in a matter of days gave me the strength and determination I lacked before to beat this setback. *'This time we were going to be as close to perfect as possible.'*

The walls were closing in on me close to a week inside. I had had enough of the facility and had to get out of there.

The receptionist summoned me to the office to take Nadia's call as I contemplated signing myself out. "Are you able to have a serious conversation right now?" she asked. I sensed trouble in her tone.

"Something is up. Are you alright?"

She hesitated and let out a deep sigh before answering. "I want to make sure we are on the same page," she said. "It's time we grow up. We've been dysfunctional long enough. Do you agree?"

"Yes. I fell off the wagon for the last time. I hope you know that. Wait a minute. I thought we already had this discussion."

"I'm just making sure we're in sync from here on out. We have to be," she emphasized.

"You called me a junkie. That's all I needed to hear to get my shit together." I huffed.

"How are you feeling?"

"Almost back to normal. And you? I can tell something's wrong. You haven't changed your mind about coming back, have you?"

"No worries, I'm coming home," she said in a strange tone of voice, then took a deep sigh. "Um, you should also know I moved out of the condo, and will spend a few days with my mother before the trip..." She paused. "Because Lucas came by the apartment, and I didn't know how to tell you. But don't be upset. I left before there was any trouble, and I'm fine. I told you I could take care of myself," she blurted quickly in one breath.

"I warned that mother...I'm on the next flight."

"No! Levi is taking care of him."

"I appreciate Levi having my back, but this doesn't concern him. This is exactly why you need to be here. With me."

"You're right."

My anger left momentarily at the sound of words I had never heard spring from Nadia's mouth. "Did you agree with me?" I choked.

"I did."

"Make sure we mark today's date and time on the calendar when we get home."

The sound of her laughter temporarily deescalated my rage. A maniac stalking her infuriated me, and I lashed out at the doctors who confused my outbursts and behavior with withdrawal symptoms. They refused to believe my rage stemmed from wanting to punch Lucas in the face again. But I knew my heart.

Completing the program was no longer my main focus, and I found myself at a crossroads— do what Nadia asked of me, or do what came naturally. Protect what was mine.

Chapter 17
Nadia

As I packed, my emotions ran high, fearing Lucas knew I was alone. His behavior rattled me. He seemed obsessed and unstable, and his domestic past made me fear for my safety when he didn't get his way.

As Olive said, he proved to be basic. I questioned everything he told me, and saw him for what he was—A random, serial pussy hound, avoiding commitment while suggesting he and Mash share me. *'Damn he almost had me.'*

As I tossed my bags into the car, I looked over my shoulders, and reflected on my stint in New York, and felt like a complete idiot. My bullshit was no better than Mash's bullshit, and I came to the realization, forgiveness has forever plagued me and served as my downfall.

Dr. Bartley told me years ago I needed to learn how to forgive myself for the mistakes I made, as well as forgive others. I purposely let her advice go over my head. I had forgiven Taylor and Isla, and reclaimed our friendship. I had forgiven Dylan and got over him, but I never forgave myself for all of the bad decisions I made.

I wasn't at peace internally because I regretted the years I spent pining after Dylan. The years I would never get back. I let his indiscretions give me insecurities because I felt he discarded me, and wasted years continuing to love him while I neglected myself. And when I learned Taylor was the reason he casted me aside, I allowed them to make me feel less than my worth, and carried the weight of their inflicted pain on me. Doubting myself, making poor choices, and most importantly forgetting who I was. *'No more.'*

I left one of my plants on the doorstep of my meddlesome neighbor, and placed the box of delivered pizza on the passenger seat. I cranked the car and left my lonely apartment in the rearview, with a new mindset to move on. I forgave myself for giving those who hurt me the power to change me. It felt good to finally arrive, as I let go of all of my baggage, and set myself free. Free to love, free to flourish, and free to be me.

Chapter 18
Lucas

Nadia was destined to be mine once I found her. We could have avoided this whole song and dance if she had stayed in New York, and not fled from her feelings for me. I felt the rush of blood flowing inside of her when I had her pinned against my wall. She was scared because of how her body responded to me. I heard the same in her voice last night.

She sounded nervous and afraid to be seen with me, but I wish her husband could see how she lights up when I'm around. Bubbly and playful, yet somehow shy. He wouldn't be able to deny our connection if he saw what she and I shared

The long months I dreamed of her pretty brown eyes staring into mine nearly happened, but I didn't plan for a screen to be between us. Refusing me access into her world when women normally give themselves to me made her stand out from the rest. Won me over, in fact. She turned the tables on me and left me hanging with a stiff rod, and I planned to show her what she was missing out on.

The hostess looked back at me twice, and heads turned when I walked into City Kitchen. I could have added many more ladies to my roster without effort, but my heart was set on Nadia. Judging from the way the ladies were on me, I was a sure thing, and I was hopeful it was a good sign she would follow suit.

While I waited for Nadia to arrive, I ordered a screwdriver and appetizers for the table. Specifically the stuffed shrimp since she loved the dish so much on 57th.

Ten minutes later the shrimp arrived, but Nadia hadn't. I finished my drink, then ordered a second when a tap on my shoulder aroused me. I turned to find two familiar faces.

"May we sit?" asked one of them, already scooting towards me in the booth.

"Please." I scowled.

"How have you been?" The other one asked, signaling for someone to come over.

"Shannon. Right?"

"No one can ever forget me," she teased.

"And you're Khai." I parted my lips.

"How have you been?" Khai coldly replied.

I responded then inquired of Nadia's whereabouts. Before they answered, a group of people squeezed into the booth. "I'm confused. Where is Nadia?"

"What's up, man? You must be Lucas." One of the fellas held out his hand.

I leaned across the table and gave him a firm handshake. "Lucas Fleming, and you are?"

"Levi, and this is my wife Taylor."

"And this is my husband Manny, and Brian, Khai's husband," said Shannon.

"Nice to meet you all I guess. Can someone tell me what is going on, and where is Nadia?"

"Nadia is...Wait a minute. Let's at least order. I'm starving. And I hear the chicken and waffles are a must have here. What did you order, my man?" said Levi.

I sat astounded by the audacity of these people turning my intimate night with Nadia into a group function. The Levi character lifted his arm and signaled for the waitress to come over.

He placed a huge order for the table, damn near everything on the front page of the menu. I sat quietly waiting for my question to be answered, and observed these people while they waited for the waitress to return with their drinks.

The Taylor woman studied me hard while the others whispered amongst themselves after tasting their concoctions. They avoided giving me an answer and included me in their small talk.

We ate and drank for nearly an hour, then Shannon asked me, "So how did you find Nadia?" The chatter at the table died down. It was then I realized I was in the lion's den.

"I know people who know people. I take it this is a test of some sort, or she isn't coming? Which one is it?"

"Be cool, man. You were real chill when we hung out before," she added.

"You all have me cornered in here, and I don't want any trouble. If you will, let me out, and I'll be on my way," I said.

"There will be no trouble. I give you my word," said Levi.

"Why are all of you here?"

"Because our good friend asked us to be." Levi replied.

"And where is your 'good friend?'"

"With my best friend. Her husband."

The waitress brought shot glasses to the table, and Levi slid one towards me. "And which one sent you? Your best friend or Nadia?" I swallowed my shot with one gulp and eyed him.

"Does it matter?" He swallowed his shot and flinched.

"It does to me. Tell your good friend I don't ever give up on revenge. If you'll excuse me, I'll be on my way."

I rose my brows for Brian to get up so I could remove myself from their company. He didn't budge.

"Everybody leave us. I'll take care of the check," Levi ordered.

The party removed themselves, and Levi and I sat across from one another testing who would be the first to blink. "Look, I know I'm the bad guy here. And yes, I'm in the wrong, but my affairs are none of your business."

"You're one hundred percent correct. But Nadia is my business. She's practically my little sister. She asked me to speak on her behalf. She wants you gone. Your persistence comes across as threatening, and so I'm asking you to please respect her wishes and leave her alone."

"She knows I wouldn't hurt her." I assured him.

"She knows about your priors. You know the domestic violence case against your wife," he said with a smug look on his face.

'Careful. You can easily catch a fist for your best friend.'

"Enough with this bullshit. Where is Nadia?" I rose my voice.

"See. You're not listening. Let my family enjoy their peace."

"Man to man. You wouldn't let another man snuff you and walk away."

"I might if I was trying to push up on his lady. You kissed his wife and he put hands on you. You had it coming. Don't lose everything you've worked hard for, over someone who wants nothing to do with you. A businessman with stalking and harassment charges— not ideal in this climate. And we all know money is power. You come nowhere close to her husband's family influence."

"His money doesn't intimidate me." I scoffed.

"It should." He warned.

I rose from the table and shook Levi's hand. "Tell Nadia if she ever changes her mind, she knows where to find me." I threw a Benjamin on the table for the tip and left.

My ass had been handed to me via third party, but I smiled on my way out of the restaurant. I had to give it to Nadia, she did her dirt classy and smart. Having me bombarded in public. What a strategist.

Every kiss we shared, including the ones I stole flashed before me as I drove away from the restaurant. I wasn't ready to let her go again, and though I said I would respect her wishes, I drove over to her place to see her one last time. "I see you came back!" Shouted the old woman in the window.

"Hello again, I don't mean to disturb you!" I shouted back.

"She isn't in there. She left with a bunch of bags. Didn't look like she was coming back if you ask me. Plus she gave our neighbor one of her plants. Didn't leave me anything!"

"I'm sure she didn't mean anything by it. I tell you what. I have some flowers in the car. I'll leave them down here for you. You take care of yourself!"

"Thank you sweetheart. If you ever need a shoulder to cry on you know where to find me!" she humorously offered.

"I sure do! Good night!"

Nadia forced me out of her life. A foreign fool was living the life with my woman, and the agony of defeat ate away at me. I drove away bursting with anger and energy, and found myself at the strip club from the week before.

I paid the whore who serviced me last time three hundred dollars to leave and be mine for the night. We went back to my hotel room, and I took my frustrations out on her gush. She dug her nails in my back while begging me not to stop. She needn't worry. I had months of built up aggression to deliver to her womb.

After I had my way with her, I threw her to the side and told her to grab her things and go. I went to the bathroom and removed the filled bag from my wood, took a piss, then turned on the water to wipe the whore off of me.

In the reflection of the mirror I noticed her rummaging through my pants. *'Typical whore, searching for more than what she earned.'*

I let the water run and snuck up on her, then held my hand out to strike her for the violation she had no time to commit. Thank goodness I wasn't completely shit-faced, or I would have gone through with it.

I lowered my hand and gave her a look of death instead. She grabbed what she could before I threw her out of my room. Half-naked on her walk of shame.

For the remainder of the night I lay wide awake, stroking my pipe, thinking of Nadia. Her sweet lips and perfect hips, unapologetically teasing my thoughts. I may not be the best man in the world, but I would have been to her. *'Damn I lost.'*

Chapter 19
Mash

Twelve days clean, and I was thinking clearly. It was too early to say I had gone cold turkey, but it was true. Nadia needed me, and that was reason enough to quit besides the fact how badly I yearned for her and her only.

With that wanker Lucas roaming about, I needed to be at her side, and out of this program. Talking once a day wasn't good enough. I worried about her safety every second I wasn't there to protect her until anxiety got the best of me.

I struggled with the notion if I was healthy and strong enough to leave every night. Then the front desk said I had a call, immediately sending my thoughts to think the worst. "How is it going in there?" asked Grams.

The biggest smile appeared on my face. Hearing her angelic voice was the sign I needed to know I was going to be okay. "It's coming along," I said, nervously nodding, her call was for the greater good.

"That makes me happy to hear. Nadia and her mother came to visit me. She told me what's been going on."

"Yeah we're working it out." I sighed.

"Good. I told Nadia no one is perfect and life always has speed bumps, but you have to keep on driving."

"Your granddaughter is in the driver's seat. I don't plan on getting out of the car if you know what I mean."

"Listen to you." She chuckled.

"How are you handling the heat?"

"Oh I'm doing mighty fine. I plan on hanging on as long as I can. Especially since my great-grandbaby is going to need me. Someone's *gotta* make sure the *youngins* coming in know the real secrets to life. You folks are too much into these computers and your devil music. It took me forever to figure out how to call you on this thing Nadia gave me. Slide up and right and foolishness."

"Nadia didn't mention her brother had another one on the way. Must have slipped her mind."

"I'm talking about you and Nadia's baby. She didn't tell me she was with child, but I dreamed I was catching fish on a lake. One look at her, and I knew."

I couldn't believe what came out of Gram's mouth. "Are you sure?" My face frowned, and my heart rate increased.

"A grandmother knows. No one can tell me different. I've been here a long time, you know."

"I love you, Grams. You're a real angel. Did you know that?"

"I've been called some things in my day, and angel ain't never been one of them." She cackled.

"Well, you are to me. I'll be seeing you real soon."

"I better." She hummed and ended the call.

Prano picked me up that evening as my busy mind jumped. I was chuffed to bits knowing my days of coming home to an empty house were numbered. News of Nadia giving me a lad of my own had me spiraling. I couldn't think of a time I was happier besides the morning I woke with her in my bed.

I prepared the house for her arrival, and as I cleaned I thought about the night she asked me to be gentle. *'I should have known then. No wonder she said it was time for us to grow up.'* Cupid really was far up her ass. With my arrow.

Chapter 20
Shannon

The pressure was on me to make this weekend perfect. Every time we went on vacations and getaways the trip went smoothly, except for California, and I wasn't about to be the one to fail.

Our home team was playing their season opener away in Miami, a *poppin'* city with much to do, so the planning was easier than I anticipated. Especially with Yohan's influence, making calls to his connects to get us on the list of the hottest venues.

We were shacked up on a beachfront luxury home, equipped with everything imaginable— two XL SUV's, swimming pool, enclosed deck, jet skis, and a secluded bonfire setup.

By sunset, just about everyone had arrived. We laid out near the bonfire while the guys barbecued on the pit, and roasted S'Mores. Not a good mix with alcohol.

The fire kept us warm from the cool breeze flowing in from the ocean. I popped in an old hip-hop mixtape to set the perfect mood of reminiscing about old times, and share stories of the good old days when we were wet behind the ears. "Throw some steaks and corn on the grill," I ordered the guys.

"Baby, we got this," Manny assured me. "You girls sit over there and let your weaves blow in the wind," he joked.

"You like pulling on this weave though." I rolled my eyes.

"Okay, you two. The night is still young and that's too much information," said Khai, calling time-out.

I ruffled her feathers further. "I'm sure Brian would love it if you let him pull on your hair, girl?" Khai glared at me and pointed her finger.

"You let me worry about my husband and mind your business," she replied.

"Why are you always so private? It's called girl talk. You can share a little something once in a while. You never contribute. Hell, you might be the OG of the group and teach us something new."

"The quiet ones truly are the freaky ones. I'm told," said Taylor. "Nadia is a quiet one, too. How are you doing over there?"

"I'm tired as hell." She dragged. "Travel takes a lot out of me these days."

"Levi was looking forward to Mash joining us. He was happy as hell y'all worked things out. Are you ready to give up all of this and abandon us again?"

Everyone listening in laughed, knowing Nadia's answer before she spoke. "Hell yeah. I miss my life over there. The fashionable yet grey vibe. Traveling in style to new places with my man. The TV shows. I almost didn't come this weekend."

"You miss your tea and crumpets," said Isla.

"She misses her hummus." I teased.

"I do miss him," she said. "Oh my God. I forgot to tell you all this. We were at lunch one day and he asked if I wanted to try the cilantro hummus on the menu. I legit had shits and giggles." Nadia's faced beamed in the light from the fire.

"Did you tell him?" I asked.

"No." She snickered. "But he kept looking at me strange because I couldn't stop cracking up."

"Why are y'all talking about hummus over there?" Manny interrupted.

We giggled as he stared at us dumbfounded.

"No reason. I forgot to buy some earlier. Is the food ready yet?" I answered.

Girl talk took a pause as we merged with the guys around the fire to eat. The songs on the mix tape brought up old memories, and created a flowing conversation allowing everyone to enjoy themselves. Until Isla opened her mouth.

"Let's play Taboo," she suggested.

"*Nooo*. You are the only here with no partner so you can't embarrass yourself," I said.

"Then how about Truth or Dare?"

My eyes shot darts in her direction. I thought to myself, '*Is this bitch dumb or something?*' "How is Truth or Dare different from Taboo?" I asked.

"Let's do it." Levi chimed in.

"How about Never Have I Ever?" Isla added.

"They are all the same. This trip is my baby. Those games start shit," I said.

"So Truth or Dare it is." Levi decided.

Sweat beads formed on most of our foreheads before the game started. We all had our fair share of secrets, side clicks, and besties, so playing an intrusive game was fifty percent fun, and fifty percent reckless. "Here are the rules," said Isla.

"We know the rules," we said in unison.

"Okay. Shannon, you are the host this weekend, so you ask the first question."

"Truth or Dare, Isla, did you break up with Evan, or did he dump you?" I demonized her with my eyes.

"Truth. He broke up with me." Isla lowered her head.

"What?!" we all screamed.

"He said he didn't want to be around our group because he felt like everyone was judging him for dating Nadia's friend."

"Please say you told him the real reason we were judging him," said Taylor.

"Which is what?" Levi asked.

The banter came to a halt while the girls and I collected ourselves. "I didn't have the heart to tell him we call him little meat," Isla said.

"Y'all call him what?" Levi stood up and ran in a circle. "You better not *say nothing* like that about me!" He pointed to Taylor.

"Enough about pencil dick. My turn. Manny, truth or dare. Is Shannon submissive when we aren't around?" Isla asked.

"Truth. She's not as boisterous at home," he answered.

"Really, babe. You were supposed to take the dare!" I chastised him.

"So you want everyone to think you run me like some chump? Nah. Now you answer a question. Did your mother tell you not to marry me?"

I looked at him dead in his eyes and grinned. "I'll take the dare." Our circle *ooh'd* and booed in between laughs.

"Wow," said Manny. "I dare you to tell Isla what you said about her the other night."

My eyes widened at the betrayal. "You must not want any action tonight." I threatened him. "I'll answer your question and still do the dare. My mother loves you, but she did not want me to marry you because athletes are known whores, and she feared I would be looking over my shoulder for the rest of my life. There. And now for the dare. Isla, I said you could find a man if you weren't so hateful. You get what you give. I still love you, though."

"Hateful?" She questioned me.

"You know you can be a certain way at times is all I'm saying. Like suggesting this game." I blinked my eyes at her nonstop and sipped on my drink.

"This is becoming toxic. Let's quit while we are ahead," Khai suggested.

"Not until we have a full round," I answered. "Khai, I pick you. Who is the breadwinner in your house?"

"Un uh, too personal. I'll take the dare."

"I dare you to drink two shots back to back."

I could have gone harder on her, but Khai was sweet. She also couldn't handle shots. "Chug chug chug chug!" We chanted.

"I hate this game." She choked and swallowed the shot.

Brian stroked her back until she caught a second wind, then whispered in Khai's ear. She called on Levi. "Levi, this one is for you. Truth or dare, what were you and Mash whispering about in Vegas?" Levi turned to Brian and lifted his hands.

"B. What kind of question is that? Your wife wasn't with us in Vegas, so why would she ask me that? New question!" he shouted. "I'm not breaking bro code," he added.

"Sounds like you are taking the dare then." Khai folded her arms.

"Go easy on me," Levi begged.

"I dare you to sit in the waves until you're soaked."

Levi headed towards the water as we cheered him on. "I thought we were cool, Khai!" he yelled, removing his shoes.

"I'm sorry!" Khai shouted.

The game took a fun turn. *'Thank God.'* Instead of sitting on the beach so the waves could soak him, Levi went in knee deep and dove into the water. We squealed and laughed as he returned to the circle completely soaked and shivering.

Khai covered him with a blanket and begged for forgiveness. Levi shook her hand and faced Brian.

"Brian, my man. The husband who will pay for the sins of his wife. Truth or dare, would you trade lives with anyone here, and if so who?"

"Truth. I would trade lives with Khai because she has it pretty damned good," Brian answered.

"No fair. You can't say your wife!" Levi mocked.

"Too late!" Brian argued.

"Group vote— I get a do over."

"As organizer of this trip, I say Levi gets to ask another question since Brian punked out with that answer," I intervened.

"New question. Who would be the worst person to date in this group?"

All eyes shifted in Brian's direction. "I'll take the dare this time," he said. Levi rubbed his hands together and grinned.

"I dare you to kiss Khai's feet with the sand on them."

Brian walked over to Khai and did more than kiss her feet. He licked both of her legs until he reached her feet, and kissed the top and bottom of them, then licked her big toe. "Don't get turned on out here," he teased his wife.

"Just ask your question so this stupid game can end," said Khai.

"Uh oh. The wife is ready to get to the bedroom." Brian joked. "Moving on. Taylor. Truth or dare. Would you give Levi a hall pass?"

"Truth. No. I'm too selfish," she answered.

"That's for damn sure," a few voices whispered.

"Last question!" I emphasized.

Taylor turned to Nadia. The circle grew quiet knowing the

history of these two was bound to bring drama. "Nadia, truth or dare. Did you sleep with the guy in New York?"

"Seriously, Taylor! What is your problem?" we all yelled.

"What?! I don't think she is telling the whole truth about that situation. That whole hiding out in Atlanta fiasco has never sat right with me. Why would that man like her so much if they didn't do anything?"

Mumbles, grunts, and teeth sucking travelled around the circle. I replied to Taylor's question first.

"Because he's vain. She's beautiful. And refused him. That's why. Some men love a challenge. He was determined to win a bet within himself."

"And like a kid, he wanted what he couldn't have," said Khai.

"And he wanted to even the score because Mash kicked his ass," said Levi.

"Thanks, y'all. It's cool. I'll answer her question. I didn't sleep with him, so you can stop wondering about it. I sure have. And don't ever bring that man up again."

"Thank God you said no," added Brian.

"Sorry to disappoint. I didn't cheat on my husband. There's no breaking news here," Nadia replied.

"That man was adamant about knowing your where-abouts," said Taylor.

"Did anyone else catch on how he never answered the question on how he found her?" Manny asked.

"Guys, I really don't want to discuss this. I've moved on with my life."

"Everybody has had a turn so let's end this game and head inside," I said.

"Oh no. I get to ask a question, then it's over," said Nadia.

The look on her face was one I recognized. The look of

petty and vengeance. Her eyes sparkled, and her lips curved on one side. Nadia's question was sure to be a kill shot.

I was sure Taylor felt the heat before the words left Nadia's mouth. We all did. She fidgeted in her seat, aware of the loaded weapon we all had against her.

The waves roared, but the beach appeared to be silent as all of our faces watched on in fear, waiting to see if Nadia was about to reveal Taylor's biggest betrayal, and finish her for good. "Taylor. Does Levi know?"

"Oh boy," I said.

"Know what?" he asked.

"Nadia," Khai whispered.

"Does Levi know what?" Taylor answered.

I shook my head side to side and muttered to Nadia, "Please don't do this now." She looked at me with sympathy, then a grin returned to her lips.

"Does Levi know what code California means?"

Myself, Khai, Isla, and even Taylor exhaled a sigh of relief. Nadia went with one of Taylor's shameful moments, and not the truth of Tyler's birth.

"You didn't say Truth or Dare," said Taylor.

"Do you really want me to start over?" Nadia threatened.

"No," Taylor replied, jittering in her chair. "Truth, the answer is no, Levi doesn't know what it means."

The sound of the waves coming ashore returned to my ears following a chorus of sighs. I told Manny the secret about Tyler's paternity, and apparently Khai had leaked the secret to Brian, too. "What is code California?" Levi asked.

"Since Isla suggested we play this ridiculous game, I think she should explain it." Nadia insisted.

"I overheard you say it once on the phone, and always wondered what it meant," Brian said to Khai.

Isla avoided eye contact with the group and stared into the

fire. Nadia tapped her feet and ended the awkward silence. "Well, if Isla doesn't want to, I certainly can," she cattily remarked.

"Sorry, Taylor. So, during our last year of college we took a trip to L.A. Taylor met this guy during Freak-Nik who promised to show us a good time if we ever came out west. He was some rich kid whose parents lived in Beverly Hills, and their main house had a guest house in the back. Taylor stayed in the main house with him, while the rest of us huddled together out back. Until things turned weird. The guy came in our room over in the night and licked Khai's face and mine while we were sleeping. I was so shook I couldn't go back to sleep. In the morning, Khai and I told the girls. Taylor swore we were making it up because we were jealous."

"That sounds about right," said Levi.

"The next day he took us shopping in this ritzy area. Nadia was pressed to go in this expensive store and try on a dress she saw in the window. She got stuck in it and couldn't get it off. We all took turns tugging at it until it became comical. You had to be there to see how bent over she was. Anyway, we came up with code California if we ever got into a situation we needed help getting out of. Little did we know we would be using the code word sooner than later. We went back to the house, and the crazy dude promised he had friends coming over for a pool party he wanted to throw for us. Khai and myself refused to sleep another night in that house, so we packed up everybody's stuff."

"And left I presume?" Brian asked.

"Not quite. Taylor and Shannon took some pills the guy gave them and lost their minds. They were so out of sorts, they didn't realize hours had went by and not one of this guy's friends ever showed up. So Khai asked him, "When are your friends supposed to get here?" This fool said, "They are already here and pulled his dick out."

"What?!" the guys shrieked.

"No lie. The joke is, when he and Taylor would talk on the phone, he kept saying he had a dick of gold. We all thought he was bragging like most men do. But he literally meant it. This nut job had a glowing gold penis and said to us, "Meet my friends Willie and his partners Dingle and Dangle. Which one of you bitches is hopping on first?" All of us screamed, "California!" and hauled ass to the car. Except for Taylor. She was so high we had to wrestle that weirdo to let her go. We found a cheap hotel, huddled up in one room, and got the hell out of California. That is how code California came about."

"Do me a favor. Don't tell anyone else that story. It takes away the sexiness of the group," Manny joked.

"A glowing gold penis?" Brian asked.

"We don't know if he spray painted it, or dipped it. All I know is we didn't talk for a long time in the car until Shannon's high came down and said, "Was I the only person to see a gold penis today?" We laughed like hyenas.

"Weirdest trip ever," said Isla.

"Are we even now Nadia?" Taylor asked.

"Never," she replied.

I rerouted everyone inside to cut the tension and noticed everyone was laughing about *goldie* except Levi. "I'm going to take a walk. I'll see y'all back inside," he said.

"Take a walk where?" Taylor asked.

Levi walked off and didn't answer. I pulled Isla to the side. "Don't make any more suggestions this weekend." She shrugged free from my grip and scoffed.

The damage was done. By the time I made it inside, Manny and Brian were in the den watching sports news, Nadia and

Khai turned in early, and Taylor and Isla sat at the bar whispering near the kitchen.

Levi found his way back to the house and gave Taylor a dirty look. "I'm calling it a night, guys," he said. Taylor followed him into their bedroom and closed the door, but we could hear their argument through the walls. "I feel like I was duped," he said. "I have no idea who you are!"

"How can you be mad at me for something so long ago? It's called being young and stupid for a reason."

"You're a big liar, Taylor! You lie so much, you have no idea why that story pissed me off! Do you?!"

"A liar?"

"I remember your trip to California. I gave you money to go on that trip. And you used it to go see a dick painting freak!"

"Like you didn't *do shit wrong* when you were young!"

"Of course I did! But not scheme money out of you to go fuck some other girl! You should be mad at yourself right now. Your envy is showing. If you hadn't asked Nadia such a dumb ass question, what happened in California would still be a secret among you and your friends. And I'd still be walking around like the sapsucker of the year. And why does it seem everyone was relieved Nadia didn't ask that second question?"

"What am I a mind reader now?"

"No. Just a liar."

"You holier than thou motherfucker!"

"I'm not holy. Everyone has a past, but you...You...Yours has a lot of color in it. I wish I knew this before..."

"Before what? Before you married me! That's what you're thinking, right?!"

"Let's call it a night."

Taylor continued to yell, but Levi remained silent. I turned to Isla. "Thanks for ruining the weekend before it ever started,"

I said, and joined Manny in my quarters. Khai knocked on my door and I followed her into the hallway.

"I totally forgot Taylor was dating Levi when we went out west," she whispered.

"But Nadia didn't forget."

"Let's go check on her."

We barged into Nadia's room and shut the door behind us. "I heard everything all the way up here," she said.

"I'm so pissed right now. I had this weekend planned perfectly and now it's all going to shits because of a stupid game," I complained.

"I thought you were about to reveal Dylan was... you know. I totally forgot they were seeing each other back then," Khai admitted.

"I'm tired of Taylor *punking* me. She had no right bringing up Lucas. What if Mash was here?"

"Nadia has a point. I'm going to check her. But not tonight because Levi is doing a pretty good job of it."

"I'd bet money she wants to pursue him. She just doesn't know how."

Khai and I shared a look. "You agree with me don't you?" Nadia smirked.

"She was studying him hard at the restaurant."

"If I didn't love Levi like my own brother, I would have brought up the baby, but I don't want to hurt him like that."

"I was relieved you didn't." I sighed. "I could ring Isla's neck right now. Tonight is a disaster because of her."

"Shannon, don't be mad, but I'm thinking about flying out in the morning," said Nadia. "I should be with my husband."

"Nope. You can't leave."

Isla and Taylor waltzed in Nadia's room. "What are y'all talking about in here?"

"The noise complaint going on my renter's record," I said.

"I'm sorry the weekend got off to a rough start, but we can turn it around in the morning," said Isla. "To make it up to everyone, I'm going to cook breakfast, mix mimosas, and give a formal apology to the entire group."

"I'm good on apologies. I'm leaving in the morning," said Nadia.

"Why is that necessary? Since everyone is upset with me, I'll leave," said Taylor.

"It's not a competition," Nadia added.

Taylor looked as if Nadia snatched her wig and ran off with it. "What do you mean by that?"

"I think you know. And don't push me further." Nadia's face turned to stone. "You're lucky I kept my mouth shut out there. And don't act all tough. You were scared to death I was about to tell your little secret. And I should have. You slept with Dylan behind my back, tried to sway me into not being with Mash, and now you bring up Lucas for no reason at all. I should have asked youTruth or Dare, do you want to fuck Lucas?"

"Nadia! What has gotten into you?" said Khai.

"I do not want to sleep with your stalker!"

"Then why would you ask me that question? Go ahead and admit it. You want to add him to your rotation. Right? Be real with me for once. You either secretly hate me, or secretly wanna be me. Which is it?"

As I clutched my fake pearls, I met eyes with every one of us present for this lashing. One of Khai's hands draped her chest and the other held onto Nadia's arm as she sat with her mouth open. Isla's eyes were so big they nearly popped out of the socket and her hands covered her mouth. Nadia sat stone faced and surly with pressed lips and narrowing eyes. And Taylor stood next to me at the foot of the bed with eyes zeroed in and stuck in headlights like a deer. "Girl, the devil has gotten into you!" Taylor screamed, and lunged towards Nadia on the bed.

Nadia lunged forward and swung upward as I pulled Taylor back. Khai grabbed Nadia and pinned her to the bed. "I am not the jealous type!" Taylor screamed continuously.

The guys burst into Nadia's room and broke up the feud. "Taylor!" Levi screamed. "Stop shouting. Let's go to bed," he said, and removed Taylor from the room.

"I don't know what happened in here, but let's break up the *Bad Girls Club*," said Manny. "You all are ruining my baby's hard work. Sleep it off. We'll reset in the morning."

You could hear crickets on Taylor and Levi's side of the house. Not the case on my side. The football coach came and rectified the mess and deserved to be rewarded. We sounded like a Midwestern compound with headboards banging against the wall, mattresses squeaking, and screams of passion from our room.

Khai and Brian attempted to keep up, but the surprise came from Isla's room. Manny and I laughed ourselves to sleep at how good she was handling her business—herself.

In the morning I greeted her in the kitchen. "Make sure you wash those hands before you cook our breakfast." I teased. She nudged me and blushed of embarrassment. I raised my eyebrows to let her know I was serious.

Nadia came downstairs with her bags in tow. I convinced her to eat with us, and had Manny take them back up to her room.

As promised, Isla delivered a lengthy apology and fed us a mediocre breakfast which explained why she was still single. The tension was still present amongst us, so before we headed into the city, I pulled the girls out to the deck to talk things out. "If I have to buy sage sticks while we're in the city, say so now because we have to fix this disconnect. It's gone on for too long," I said. "Isla and Taylor, you both started this. Isla we accept your apology. Taylor, you instigated this feud with your question. I can't make you apologize. But you were wrong. Nadia..."

"I have a flight to catch." She interrupted my spill.

"I was going to say, You retaliated with the California story within reason, and also, I hope you got everything off of your chest last night because whew." I wiped my forehead. "That was a lot to take in."

"Everyone asked personal questions last night," Taylor said.

Accountability, Taylor. Look it up," said Khai. "Your question was out of line. You need to apologize so we can move on."

"As always, the room is against me."

"The only way we are going to solve this is to get to the root of the problem. What is it?" Khai asked.

Nadia folded her arms and Taylor bit her nails. I looked to Isla and Khai. "Do either of you know?" They both shrugged their shoulders.

"Nadia thinks she is better than me, and frankly I'm sick of it. She's gotten worse since London. You all didn't see how she was acting at his house, and frankly I didn't think it was fair of you to steal the spotlight on my wedding weekend— Hooking up with a stranger, all lovey dovey, when I was going through what I was going through."

"I didn't tell you to hook up with my ex."

"There it is. The judgement."

"You can't blame me for your guilt. You're miserable, and it has nothing to do with me."

"I also think you and Levi are a little too close for my taste."

"That is rich coming from you of all people."

"There it is again. The *judgey* face."

"Because you sound crazy. Levi is like a brother to me. You are creating shit about me in your head, and I don't know why."

"Because I'm not happy, like you said. Okay. Levi used to say Dylan wasn't good enough for you. I wonder if he would say the same thing about him not being good enough for me."

"Taylor, no one told you to fuck that loser," Nadia whispered with a sarcastic grin on her face.

"I don't know what I'm doing. I'm not happy."

"Because you love Dylan. Am I right?"

"I do."

"Then be with him, and set Levi free to find the happiness he deserves. He's too good of a man to be treated this way. I meant what I said in New York. I have no feelings or concern for Dylan whatsoever. He is your son's father. Go be a family if that's what you want. Just know what you're doing, 'cause going from Levi to Dylan is going from sugar to shit."

"But please don't do it this weekend," I begged.

Taylor looked aloof with tears in her eyes. A breeze floated upwards to the deck, and we all exhaled. "If I leave Levi for Dylan, I'll be alienating myself from you all," Taylor confessed.

"No shade, but Mash and I said we would get Levi in the divorce."

"There it is. The holier than thou attitude."

"I said no shade. I was trying to be funny but also tell the truth. You're worried about the wrong things. You should be focused on your son."

Chapter 21
Nadia

Shannon convinced me to stay against my wishes. We went into town and explored the city, enjoying a spa day at the grand opening of To The Max.

I was pampered like the name of the salon, then had my makeup done by a lovely girl named Jen Carson, an artist whose talent hid the bags under my eyes, and brought out the glow buried beneath the stress on my skin. "Your secret is safe with me," she said when I sat in her chair.

"I beg your pardon?"

"I overheard your friends talking about going out later on. I can tell from the way your neck is jumping, you'd rather be off of your feet and taking it easy." She winked. "Don't worry. I'll make sure you look better than them tonight. I'm the best artist in here."

"Is that so?"

"Well, I should be. It is my place after all." She gloated.

"Congratulations. I admire successful women. Make sure you give me your card. I'm venturing out and could use a makeup artist with your skills the day I hit the red carpet."

She slipped me her card and escorted me to the lounge where Shannon revealed her big surprise. "When we get back to the house, put on your shades of blue you were asked to pack. We are going out on the water tonight."

We followed our orders and met downstairs. The path outback was lit by glass covered candles, leading the way in the weed covered sand and seashells to the pier. Squeals of excitement were drowned by the sounds of the ocean as we crossed the gangway and boarded a yacht Shannon rented for an evening tour of Miami's coast.

She led us to the top, fully catered with a spread of the many flavors of Miami, and another surprise on the outer deck. "Oh My God!" I shouted, jumping into the arms of Mash.

The sight of him sent me into my own private world. We made out like we were behind closed doors. "Do you have something to tell me?" He raised his brows and smiled.

"How did you know?"

"Grams called me, and I immediately came to be by your side. Tell me it's true." His eyes never looked happier.

"Yes. I'm having your baby," I said. "I never could get anything past Grams."

"Do they know?"

"I haven't said a word to anyone. I thought you should know first."

"Give me those lips one more time." He kissed me, filling me with a burst of energy. "She's having my baby!"

Congratulations came from all aboard minus one, but the different shades of blue outweighed the minor green. The mood on the water was serene as we circled a small distance not far from the house. We danced, we ate, we drank, and we laughed, then scattered off into sections while the men smoked cigars on the balcony.

Isla pointed out yet again, she was the only single person on the boat. "I'll ask Levi to hook you up with Drew," I suggested.

"He was going to come this weekend, but something happened with his company. He may show up to the game, but honestly, I hope he doesn't. I'm going to need a partner to live the single life with," said Taylor.

"You two didn't make up last night?" Isla grabbed Taylor's hand.

"We haven't said two words to one another all day. It is what it is. But enough about me, let's talk about this baby. I should have known something was up. You were way harsh last night."

"Blame it on the hormones."

'That would be Taylor saying congratulations.'

"How far along are you?" Shannon asked.

"Three months this weekend."

"Which one of us will be the godmother? You better not say Olive." Shannon pouted.

"All of you, of course. And speaking of Olive, she knows about Yohan's philandering ways."

"Does she know about me?"

"Only by moniker. You're either Thunder Thighs, Good Good, or RT3."

"Did he really put RT3 in his phone? I'm so flattered." Shannon blushed.

"You're RT3? What does it mean?"

Shannon giggled to herself. Shrieked to herself. And rocked her shoulders side to side. She looked over her shoulder then confessed. "Yohan does this thing that drives me insane. I've been trying to get Manny to do it, but he won't budge. Let's just say, he gives the best oral care I've ever experienced." She held up her finger. "But also, he goes back down on me after we've arrived, and licks me from the Rooter To The Tooter. RT3."

I fanned myself while Isla verified the details. "He does it every time?" she asked.

"Every time." Shannon grinned.

"I might mention that to Brian." Khai rose her brows and grinned.

We laughed at Khai's sudden freaky freedom flag blowing in the wind, then ended two hours of treading in the water. Still wound from the cosmic energy of the ocean, the house felt serene when we returned, and the night was spent filling the house with screeching mattresses, muffled pillow moans, and relentless orgasms coming from all of the rooms. Especially ours.

Chapter 22
Mash

My time in the air felt like a lifetime. I was in a hurry to feel Nadia's stomach, look into her eyes, and see myself in them when she confirmed a part of me was growing inside of her.

During the layover I grew anxious, but my nerves eventually settled once the plane took off and circled the Miami skyline.

The end of summer in the southern U.S. was significantly different than it was back in London. I had to peel off layers before we landed, then took a cab to the house. The driver studied me in the rearview as I appeared crazy, smiling on and off to myself. But I didn't care who stared or judged me. The past few months had been shit, and I was in need of this reunion.

I checked the time incessantly, waiting to see them march from the house onto the pier. Nadia was close, and I could feel her in my arms before she arrived on the boat. I couldn't wait for her to see me sober.

Her silhouette stuck out to me as soon as she stepped onto the deck, and the shade of blue she wore reminded me of our first date. I envisioned the way she looked the night we stood outside of Buckingham Palace and grinned to myself. She knew she was irresistible in blue. She knew wearing that color that night would make me desire her. And she was right.

Her skin glistened in the moonlight that night, and in rehab I imagined her lips kissing mine, and how she looked when she said, "We can go to your house."

The air was cool, but I wasn't. I was nervous when footsteps echoed aboard. I waited on the upper deck like Shannon instructed me with sweaty palms the closer high heels tapped coming up the steps. Finally, there she was. Me in these navy khakis, and my Nadia, luminous in cobalt. Pure radiance bottled in the silkiest chocolate skin. I could smell her fragrance sweeping towards me before she jumped into my arms, and I held her close, listening for a second heartbeat.

The breeze was steady but we embraced so tightly, our skin formed sweat beads from the heat between us. I kissed her honeyed lips then showed her off to everyone aboard and announced, "She's having my baby!"

Our friends applauded and interrupted our embrace with their own, then I made my way back to her. I wanted to keep my hands on her tiny hardened bump, but the fellas pulled me away to celebrate.

Levi congratulated me and passed around cigars for all the guys, but I could tell he had other things on his mind. "Look at you planting seeds." He tapped my chest with the back of his hand. "This is what you two needed. You were about to throw away a good thing."

"A magnificent thing," I added. "I'm so happy, man. What about you? How are things going?"

"Terrible. Be glad you got here a day late. I'm sure Nadia will catch you up. By chance do you know what code California means?"

"Ugh, yeah. Nadia told me during pillow talk one night." I sighed.

"Well, I learned about it last night."

We both raised our eyebrows and puffed our cigars. "Speaking of codes, do you know why the word hummus is so humorous?" I asked.

"I can't say I do." Levi sucked his teeth. "These women and their secrets. If it wasn't for Tyler, I would have filed for divorce a while ago. I have no idea who I'm married to. A new start might do me some good."

"Nadia and I go to the gym and box. You two should try it." I suggested.

"We would kill each other," he said, then led us in laughter.

"Then spend some time on my side of the world."

"I just might. You owe me one anyway. I dealt with ole boy for you." He shook his head.

"He's a prat." I seethed through my teeth.

"If that means a motherfucker, then you hit it on the nail. I see why you clocked his ass. He had it coming."

We finished our cigars and headed back inside with the ladies. I pulled Nadia away, and we tucked in a corner on the upper balcony. Her hair tickled my nose as I kept her warm, draping my arms around her.

I was on a natural high, following her around like the puppy she once claimed to be, and pounced on her with lightning speed when the boat docked and brought the evening to a close.

We had some making up to do. I was wild with desire, but afraid to unleash like the beast inside of me. Nadia, on the other hand, begged for the savage to come out. "I've been waiting for this all night," she said, gripping my wood at the tip. I caved immediately.

She mumbled indistinctly, but I wasn't listening. Her swirling tongue had all of my attention, sucking me front to back, up and down, and around my shaft to the bell-end. She bodied me intentionally so I wouldn't take long, and when she rose, she turned her back to me, spread her ass open, and invited me inside her warm walls. "I'm ready," she whispered.

"You're always ready," I teased. "Tell me if I go too deep," I warned her, and slowly slipped inside. "I don't want to hurt you."

"I'll tell you if you do. I missed you so much," she said, reaching back. "Now stop playing with me and put it all in," she demanded.

I followed her command, and she shivered like a train was going past the house. I wasn't far behind. My sweet was dripping wet, throbbing around my cock. I stroked deep and slow nonstop, fighting the urge to let loose like a canon. "*How you doing, my love?*" I asked.

"Mmm hmm," she moaned.

"I'm about to--"

"Go ahead, I'll get you back up," she cut me off.

Her feet tucked below my thighs as she bounced and squeezed. I whimpered. When she rode me with such intense, orchestrated grips, I always shot quicker. Especially when her folds pressed against me in a back shot. "Yes!" she shrieked. "I feel your head swelling. Let it out, big boy."

When Nadia talked dirty to me, I was over. I stroked her harder, and she gasped softly under her breath. I lost control and plunged my way into orgasmic delight, gripping her waist and pulling her back next to my chest. My fingers travelled forward and held her belly. "Is everything alright in there?" I asked, kissing her shoulder. She turned around and nodded, then kissed my lips as our souls spoke to one another. I was complete.

Chapter 23
Levi

The suite at the stadium was big enough for us to spread out and not be huddled under one another. I hadn't spoken to Taylor since our shameful display at the house Friday night, and my disdain for her put me in the familiar space of withdrawal when I learned about her affair. I buried the hurt and shame she brought upon me once. But after hearing about her shenanigans from early on, I accepted our marriage was an expensive sham.

I pretended to enjoy the game until Taylor's lying hazel eyes rested upon me. I had to get out of there before I further embarrassed myself. "We're winning by a landslide," I said. "I'm gonna step out and check out the shops. Maybe tailgate for a bit."

"I'll come with you. My cousins have a spot somewhere outside." Brian invited himself along.

The conversation with Brian was dry while we waited for the elevator. It arrived filled to capacity, forcing us to stand longer with a struggling conversation. "Are you sure it's cool I joined you?" Brian asked. "You seem like you need some time to yourself. Matter of fact, I'll go find my people's tent, and you can call me if you want to catch up."

"I was never going to the shops, B. I think I'll follow you and see what your fam has going on."

The elevator returned and took us down to the ground level. We sifted through the crowds to exit the gate, comfortable to speak freely with significant distance from the suite. "Let's find these fools so we can get you toasted and relaxed. Cheer up, man. You two will be alright. We've all had fights. That's marriage. It comes with being domesticated, I suppose."

"Easy for you to say. You're not the one in it." I huffed, uninterested in his opinion on the matter.

"True, but the past is the past. I admit I would be angry hearing about Khai and some other guy. But I'd also let it go. We have to. We're married."

"It appears only one of us is married in my house, B. Has Khai shared Taylor's little secret with you?"

Brian's face grimaced, and his shoulders tensed. He didn't have to answer verbally. I knew he knew. "I've never stepped out on my wife. And I could have several times. Even after we married. But the image of her being with someone else is recurrent in my head. I thought my being faithful would warrant the same in return. You know?"

"I've had my share of advances. Before and after Khai and I were married. When we were dating, I almost lost her, though. I was still playing around, and Khai grew suspicious and cut me off. We split for a while, then one night I saw her out with some cat. She was smiling a little too much with him, and I didn't like that shit. I had to tighten up and get her back," he confessed.

"How did you do it?"

"I went over and pulled up a chair to their table and told dude we had unfinished business."

"Say word."

"Word. I pulled out some cash and paid for their dinner and told him to leave. The rest is history."

"And how did you get past her you know...with ole boy?"

"Khai wasn't an easy lay, so in my mind I stopped it in time. Plus, I wasn't innocent, so I never asked and let it go."

"Do you ever hear from those other girls?"

"Yeah. One follows me online. Liking my pictures and shit. The other got married and invited me to the wedding. I wish you well, Ms. Thang, but I'm not coming to that shit." He cackled.

Brian gave me the laugh I needed to lighten up as we entered the wild and loud tailgating section. The aroma of mesquite, smoked food, tent-filled fans shouting at one another, and friendly camaraderie surrounded us.

Some folks wearing our team colors invited us over to join them for beers, and to taste their cook's special sauce. "Are y'all from the Queen City?" The cook's wife asked.

"Born and raised," Brian answered.

"Then help yourself to some barbecue. We have plenty," she offered.

"The beer is enough for me," I replied.

"I insist," the cook said. "My ribs are the best you'll ever try, and I look forward to you guys spreading the word about us back home. My sauce will be in stores soon."

We partook with their blessings and lost track of time, thanks to crowded conversations about our team's defense being the best in the league, the grill master's business plan, and wiping sauce from the sides of our mouths.

Khai called and summoned Brian back to the suite before we found his cousin's tent. "You go ahead without me. I'm going to hang out here for a little while longer," I told him.

I stayed in the tent and chatted with the chef long enough

to taste the fresh slabs of ribs coming off of the grill. The tenderness and flavor had me hooked.

He gained a new customer, and I gained a new investment. After collecting his business card, I checked the status of the game. It was the end of the third quarter. I had overstayed my welcome with the grill master, and couldn't bring myself to return to the suite. I caught a taxi back to the house, packed my bags, and left Miami.

Taylor was livid I abandoned her. I could have handled my exit better, but for once I didn't think about her feelings. I thought about mine. And with the house to myself, I searched through her personal belongings. I went through coat pockets, purse zippers, and shoe boxes, and found nothing.

My father-in-law called to scold me, then I continued with my raid, checking Tyler's room for something to prove the feeling I had in my gut was right. After coming up empty handed, I gave up. Realizing I wasted the morning on a witch hunt, for Taylor's secrets were well kept.

I regrouped and grabbed a blanket from the chest and Tyler's favorite toy from his bed, then picked up my boy from my parent's house. We came back home after a half hour at the park, then I put him down for a nap. I watched him sleep trying to figure out how I was going to face his mother when her flight landed. Then it dawned on me. I didn't look under his bed.

I fumbled beneath the mattress while Tyler napped. He slept while I wiggled my forearm until my fingers felt a pointed edge. I assumed it was a loose spring and lifted the bed slightly to get a better view. The springs were all intact, and the pricking came from a sealed envelope addressed to Tyler.

I opened it, and read:

My dear boy,

Blend

It's your first birthday & I'm sorry I'm not there. Your mother and I have a lot of explaining to do when you get older, but I didn't want you to ever think I didn't want to be in your life. You mean the world to me. You come from a long line of broken households, and I didn't want this for you. When you are of age I will be waiting to do all the things I have imagined we would do together. Happy birthday. My first born son. I love you.
    Your Dad

I seethed with rage. "Damn!" I shouted and woke the baby. I rubbed his back and put him back to sleep, then read the letter a second time in disbelief of the words. '*Who was this joker writing this letter to my boy?*' I wondered.

I looked at Tyler closely as he slept peacefully like the angel he is, and my mind drew another picture as a whirlwind of thoughts bombarded me. It broke my heart to think he wasn't mine, revealing the hidden violence in my bones as I punched a hole in the wall.

In the morning, I patched the hole and covered it with a photo waiting to be hung from the garage, then scheduled a paternity test.

As expected, Taylor arrived home ready to fight— yelling and cursing without any consideration of the baby. When she paused to catch her breath, I responded, "Tyler has already had a bath, and is sleeping. I'll be back in the morning for my things."

She followed me to the garage, slapping me, and kicking my car until I pulled out of the driveway. I looked at her one last time from my rearview, then grinned to myself when her shoe hit my window. I shook my head, then drove off, wishing my window was down so I could have taken her pump with me to piss her off further.

My night at a hotel near my office turned out to be a waste of money. Unable to sleep, I went to work earlier than normal, and watched the minutes turn on the clock. When it was time for the appointment, I scooped my boy from daycare and submitted to the paternity test— sick to my stomach.

We waited for Taylor to make it home in the foyer. Tyler was playing at my feet when she walked in ready to argue once again. She rolled her eyes at my luggage sitting at the door. "I see you don't plan on spending the night at home again," she said, blinking incessantly.

"Who is Tyler's father?" I asked.

"Come again?" She choked on her saliva.

"You've been busy, Taylor. Stop with the lies. Be a woman and tell me the truth for once. Who is he?"

"Where is this coming from?" She looked dumbfounded.

"You have been lying to me from the moment I met you. I saw the text on our honeymoon. You were seeing someone else while we were engaged."

"Levi."

"Do you even know who the father is? How many tricks have you been..."

She held up her hand. "Let me stop you right there. Don't sit over there and act all high and mighty with me. If you saw the text, why didn't you say anything?"

"Because I forgave you. I fooled myself to believe you were ending your affair, and taking our marriage seriously. How silly of me to think about the money we spent, and the embarrassment of calling it quits on the honeymoon. What were my friends going to think? What were my parents going to think, who warned me you were a little shifty and needed too much attention? I should have gotten an annulment when we made it home," I decreed.

"I wish you would have."

"So we agree, this is over. Now tell me. Who is his father? I know he isn't mine."

Her eyes turned pinkish in the corners with red dots forming like lasers. She held her lips tight and balled her fists. I braced myself to take more blows , determined not to leave until she answered me. "The test results say 0%," I said.

Her eyes dilated bigger than a coin. "I can't believe you had my baby tested behind my back."

"You don't have a leg to stand on when it comes to doing shit behind someone's back. Who is the father?!"

"It's Dylan!" she answered with a poisonous tongue and grin across her lips.

"Nadia's Dylan?" I confirmed in a high pitch tone.

"What do you mean 'Nadia's Dylan?'" Her eyes narrowed, lips pouted, and wiped the grin off of her face.

"Is he who you were texting on our honeymoon?"

"Yes."

A wicked laugh left my lips. I exhaled deeply and sucked my teeth. "You can have the house. If you can afford it. How many of our friends know?"

She huffed and folded her arms. "Have you ever had a thing for Nadia? I deserve to know after all these years."

"I wish I could hurt you right now and say yes, but the answer to your ridiculous question is no. You have always been jealous of her. And now you and her ex-boyfriend share a child. The boyfriend who treated her like shit, may I add. What a friend you are. Good luck to you." I chuckled on my way out.

"Get the hell out, Levi!"

She startled Tyler. I picked him up from the floor and kissed his cheeks. He laid his head on my shoulder, and I rubbed his back and whispered calmly in his ear.

"Give him to me!" Taylor continued to shout.

"I know he's not mine, but I'm not giving him to you until you calm down."

I pacified him in my arms while Taylor looked on with pure hatred for me in her eyes. He sucked on his finger and gripped tightly on my shirt. I sat with him and talked to him softly, holding back the tears in my eyes. "I don't want to leave him with you like this. Call your mother and see if he can spend the night with her until you get yourself settled."

She stomped out of the room, mumbling indistinctly. I sat with Tyler until my in-laws arrived, kissed Tyler goodbye, and carried my bags to my car. My father-in-law followed me outside. "What's going on here, son?" he inquired.

"I'm sure Taylor wants to give you her side of the story," I replied respectfully.

"But I'm asking you."

"We have called it."

"Son, we spent a lot of money on the wedding. How can you walk away from your family so easily?"

"Tyler is not my son," I announced stone faced.

"Say what?"

"You've been a great father to me, sir. But I have to get going."

We shook hands, and I drove away with shattered dreams. The tears I held back finally fell when the loneliness settled in, and the images of Taylor and Dylan agitated me through a sleepless night.

I agonized for weeks. The wife I adored stole my options, my dignity, and my son. Teaching me a valuable life lesson. Love can quickly turn into hate, and this was now my reality.

Chapter 24
Nadia

The holidays were difficult for some of us. Levi especially. Mash and I insisted he join us at Yohan and Olive's New Year's Eve Bash. It was the perfect way to thank him for fixing my Fleming Foul.

Olive did me a solid and introduced him to some of her friends. I didn't know who he ended up connecting with, but needless to say he was occupied for days after the party.

A few weeks later, we met the gang, minus Taylor, in Utah for the premiere showing of my short film Yohan brought to life. I was in the beginning of my last trimester, stretching out my sweaters and absorbing confidence from everyone who came to support.

An unlikely fivesome, Olive, Khai, Shannon, Isla and myself met in a bistro down from the hotel. It was the buffer space I needed to test Shannon's behavior around Olive. I led with, "Did you three drive Manny crazy on the plane?"

"He's flying in later on tonight." Shannon smirked at me.

I quickly grew nervous.

"Look at you. You can't hide your stomach anymore," she deflected.

"I know. I tried for as long as I could. You all met Olive in Paris, right?"

"Hello." Shannon leaned over and hugged Olive. "Yeah we met at one of those parties. How are you?"

"Happy to get a change of scenery, but not happy to still be in the cold. I'm long overdue for some sun." Olive shivered.

"I couldn't agree with you more," said Shannon. "We all should visit someplace tropical before the baby gets here."

Khai and I side-eyed Shannon. She was handling the presence of Yohan's leading lady better than I had expected, and testing my nerves with her sneaky motives. My eyes shifted towards Olive, sitting at the end of the table clueless she was in the presence of RT3. My chest burned from betrayal.

"Yohan reserved a room at a cigar club tonight. Will your significant other arrive in time to join them?" Olive asked Shannon.

"My husband should be arriving no later than seven o'clock," she replied.

"Great. He'll have plenty of time to settle in and join them. As for us divas, I booked an extra room and have a special night of pampering, amenities, and entertainment planned. You're all invited. I won't take no for an answer." She stared each of us in the eyes.

"We would love to," Shannon answered for us.

"Great. I'll see you all then. Ciao." Olive waved as she strutted out of the bistro.

"*Ciao.*" Shannon frowned and mocked her.

I braced myself for whatever was about to fly from Shannon's mouth. "What shall my excuse be for not attending that shit?" Shannon said.

"Oh, you're going," Khai replied. "We are keeping a close eye on you this weekend."

"Please." Shannon placed the back of her palm in front of her face. "You all know if I want to do something, I'm going to do it."

"How, with your husband in town?" I asked.

"Not to mention he's going to be smoking cigars with Yohan tonight."

"I've held up my end of the bargain. I was nice to your little friend. How did I do?"

I glared at Shannon and huffed. "You really make me uncomfortable," I said. Shannon stuck her tongue out at me and Isla chimed in.

"Taylor asked me to pass along her well wishes for you this weekend."

"I would have invited her, but Levi is here, and I think I have the right to be selfish this weekend. No drama," I said looking back at Shannon. "She said she would only come if Dylan was welcome. So, of course, I told her we would see her on the next one."

"I wish I knew what direction they were headed in. I definitely would have left him home this weekend if I was her. But hey. She continues to dig herself in a hole." Isla scrunched her lips.

"Especially when he refused to move in together," Khai added.

"Yes!!!" Isla's voice travelled past our table. "I confronted him, and to be honest, the brother is plain shady. He caused this woman to lose her friend, her husband, and her house. He wouldn't shack up to help with the baby full time, and wouldn't confirm if the rumors were true about him throwing and catching, so now he might be risking her health." Isla paused to catch her breath.

"What?!" We all gasped.

"I heard that rumor, but they say it about everybody these days." Shannon shrugged her shoulders.

With the conversation going from one extreme to the next, we wrapped up lunch and strolled through the exhibits, then stopped by a day party Mash was working.

They stayed at the party when I left to meet Yohan to prepare for our Q&A session, completely exhausted with no time to rest as I met up with the ladies in Olive's reserved suite.

Shirtless men opened the door, served trays of food and champagne, and danced in corners. "I may have misjudged Ms. Olive," Shannon whispered.

"Does this mean you're going to stop cheating with her man?" Isla asked.

Shannon ignored the question and grooved to the music in the background. "Look, our host is about to speak." She smirked.

"Welcome to The Olive Hour. Drink, eat, and enjoy that of your choosing this evening. On my soon to be husband's dime." She laughed.

More shirtless men walked from the back of the suite. She had male manicurists, masseuses, estheticians, and make-up artists divided into sections of the room. "I have to give it to your new best friend. She knows how to live this lifestyle," Shannon whispered in my ear. A certain sadness could be heard in her voice, and her eyes didn't shine with mischief as they had in the bistro.

Olive planned the perfect way to spend opening night at the festival, and surprised everyone in attendance with a designer clutch bag full of luxury samples and gift cards. The wait staff turned into exotic dancers once the pampering was complete, and when the fun was all over, she announced the get together was actually her bachelorette party. "Yohan and I are eloping in Vegas after the festival!"

I glimpsed at Shannon, wearing her poker face as I congratulated Olive. "Why didn't you tell me you two were doing the Vegas thing?" I asked.

"He sprung it on me as we boarded the plane. I put this shindig together today. Of course, with the help of his team and the concierge."

"I'm happy for you two. You have to come by and tell me all about it when you return."

"I will. I'll be spending all day tomorrow fitting for a dress, so I'll miss the showing. Can you forgive me?"

"You don't need my forgiveness. You're getting married." I squeezed her hand.

The girls and I retreated to Isla's room, the only private room amongst the group. Khai asked the burning question, "Are you okay, Shannon?"

"Why wouldn't I be? I'm married. He is about to be married. It is what it is," she answered without making any eye contact, and walked out of the room.

We didn't believe her spiel. She liked Yohan more than she led on, and was bothered by the way Olive flaunted him and their wealth in front of her. "Watch her for me, please?" I asked Khai and Isla. "I need to turn in."

I was asleep when Mash strolled in. He woke me, massaging my sore feet. "Today's the big day," he said, moving his hands upward on my legs.

"I'm ready to get it over with."

"Ready to get it over with?" He frowned. "This is the just the beginning."

"I'm worried about the backlash. Could be the pregnancy talking."

Seven o'clock arrived faster than I anticipated after a day

filled with features, actor spotlights, and meet and greets. The lights dimmed in the audience, and my legs trembled forcefully. The row of chairs seated near me shook, bringing attention to my nervous face.

Yohan grabbed my knee. "I would have advised you to take a drink beforehand, but...the baby." He chuckled. "I'm removing my hand now before someone photographs it on your leg and turns this into a scandal. Then again, any publicity is good publicity," he joked, and lifted his fingers slowly. "You know I have two girlfriends in here watching me like a hawk."

I laughed at him making fun of his situation, and the vibration in my thighs slowly calmed. I pressed them together. "You mean your soon to be wife, and my friend you need to let go." I rose my brows at him, then glanced over at Shannon. "I told Shannon to end it with you."

Yohan sighed and settled in his seat. "I suspect she will after Olive's stunt with the bachelorette party. I love Olive, I do, but if I had known Shannon before, things might be different," he admitted.

"Oh God. Stop talking. I don't want to know anymore. Don't put me in the middle," I begged.

"You're such a square, Nadia." He laughed.

I made eye contact with Mash, clueless to what I was eluding to. His top lip puckered before he grinned on the side of his mouth. I shifted my eyes back towards the screen.

Hearing the audience laugh at the punch lines in my piece won me over, and the sound of clapping and cheering when the lights turned on settled my nerves.

"I knew I had a hit on my hands," said Yohan.

"I will forever be grateful you gave a newbie like me a shot." We shook hands.

"Now we go onstage and answer a few questions." He gestured the way. "Ladies first."

"Don't let me ramble," I said under my breath.

"If you're asked a question you aren't comfortable answering, do like we practiced. I'll save you."

Yohan saved me a few times during the Q&A until I was asked where I got the idea to write the short. As I stumbled in my response, the audience's stares petrified me. Shannon heckled, "Go ahead and tell them it's about me! I'm her best friend, y'all!" The audience laughed, and my speech settled.

"I wrote this out of fear I would never find my true self." I looked at Mash.

Yohan chimed in and lightened the mood. "Isn't her honesty refreshing? It's what attracted me to her work." The viewers applauded, and the session came to a close.

As I walked down the steps on the side of the stage, Mash presented me with roses and an endearing kiss. "I'm proud of you. You've arrived." He smiled. "One more thing. You have found yourself."

Yohan interrupted, "Nadia, have your entourage come to the suite for dinner. We'll head over to the after party from there."

Following orders, we met in the soon to be newlyweds' suite. Tables were shaped into two rectangles as hors d'oeuvres floated around the room to accommodate the mingling guests. Yohan tapped on his glass and toasted to our success. I blushed as clinking flutes offered us cheers, then stuffed my face on a four-course meal prepared by a world renowned chef.

Guests mingled to discuss the film after dinner was served. Mash stole my attention, lightly pinching my side. "What does this prick want?" he mumbled.

I turned to my left, greeted by Chili. "I arrived to the screening late, but I hear we got rave reviews," he said. "Congratulations."

"Yeah we did. Congratulations to you as well. You starred in it." I said through my teeth and a fake smile.

"Nice to see you both again." He placed his hand out in front of Mash. "How was your last tour? You are making some serious moves, man."

I stared Mash in the eyes until he countered with a handshake. "Yeah," Mash said, then barely embraced his hand. "Let's talk a walk."

Chili's eyes grew big. "Look, I actually came over to apologize to you both. I crossed the line and was hoping to leave all of that in the past and move forward."

"We accept," I answered.

Mash scowled at him. "My wife has apparently spoken for me. You take it easy."

"And congratulations on this, too." He pointed to my stomach.

"Thanks," Mash answered. "Glad you could make it out."

I hid my lips as Mash dismissed him, then skipped on the after party. Mash returned over in the night with bandages on his face, and bruises on his chest with the goofiest smile on his lips boasting about how he handled himself. "You should have seen the other guy," he said.

"I don't care about the other guy," I professed.

Seeing him riled up turned me on. I couldn't help myself. I initiated contact. "You feel like...you know...it's been a minute," I said.

"You know I'm worried about hurting you."

"I'll be fine. And I want it how you used to give it to me."

My God the frustration I felt having to settle for a gentle session. If I had gotten my way, I would have slept like the baby inside of me. Instead, I laid in bed rubbing on his scruff until he passed out, then traced the bruise on his chest, wondering if his temper would ever flame out.

Chapter 25
Shannon

The after party was crowded, providing an easy exit for Yohan and I to get some one on one time. Something about our dynamic shifted, but before we could figure it out, Khai began texting me **California** like a maniac.

My pants were half-zipped and my buttons undone when I said goodbye to Yogi. It felt like the final goodbye— like we knew this was the last time we were ever going to be together, but neither of us would say the words out loud. We loved each other, and whatever unspoken bond we left behind in the room, I already missed.

I sadly kissed my lover and hurried back to the party, lashing out at Khai for interrupting my rendezvous. She warned me Olive was circling the room, and I apologized for barking at her for having my back. As we were making light of the situation, Khai grabbed my arm and pointed into the crowd, "One more thing. Lucas is here."

We grabbed the guys and gathered at the side of Mash's booth. When he finished his set, he beat us to the punch and told us he saw him in the crowd, too. We were so heavily engaged with one another, none of us noticed him standing behind us. Levi stood in front of all the girls, and Mash stepped forward, "Are you stalking me now? Or are you a fanboy?"

Lucas stepped in his face. "I told you I would get my revenge. Where is baby girl?" He grinned.

Mash formed a fist, and Manny intervened. "There are ladies present, cameras all around, and heavy security. Take this outside."

"Mash. Don't do it," said Khai and Levi.

He walked over to security and whispered something in their ear, then turned around and said to Lucas, "Let's go!"

We followed Mash and the two security guards to the rear exit. Khai begged Levi and Brian to talk some sense into Mash, but he wasn't listening. He had the look of the devil in his eye when he stared at Lucas, and Lucas had the eye of the tiger in his. "Nadia told us to babysit him," Khai whispered. "We can't let him do this. It's foolish."

Not a second was wasted. Mash took off his jacket and threw the first punch, hitting Lucas in the mouth. The condensation from his mouth formed a cloud, and all the guys sounded off, "Oooooh!"

"I told you, you hit like a bitch," said Lucas.

"This guy is mad disrespectful, Mash. Hit him again," Manny ordered.

Mash was way ahead of Manny's request. He landed a second punch to Lucas's chin, causing his head to fly backwards. "You can't say that one was weak. Hell, I felt it." Manny laughed out loud.

Lucas didn't insult Mash after feeling the heat from his fists and rushed him. They tussled, exchanging blow after blow as the frozen clouds from their mouths dripped of blood. Out of nowhere, Mash landed a right hook to Lucas's ear, forcing him into the circle surrounding them.

One of the security guards asked me, "What is this all about?"

Isla happily butted in and explained, "The black one is stalking the white one's wife."

"What a way to sum it up," said Khai.

"How would you describe it?" Isla asked.

"You could have said the taller one is stalking the smaller one's wife."

"I see your point. Give me a pass. It's cold as shit out here." She turned and smiled at the security guard.

"Get him off of you, Mash!" I shouted.

"You like this, don't you?" Khai scowled at me.

"Mmm hmm. Yes. I'm enjoying this very much. Something about a man showing his strength turns me on," I replied.

"*You here* with someone?" the other security guard asked.

"Yes, she is. But I'm not." Isla smiled.

The fight took a turn, and Lucas landed some stunners to Mash's lip and cheek. He then fell backwards into the circle. The guys threw him back towards Lucas who taunted him. "I don't hear your people talking shit now. Do I?" he bragged.

"Knock his ass out, Mash!" I shouted.

Mash started moving his feet and dodging Lucas's jabs. Lucas grew winded. "Fight me, prick, or are you ready to call uncle?" Mash teased.

Lucas jabbed Mash in the chest and stomach, landing a few in a row, then missing the next couple of swings. Mash blocked some of the punches, but was pushed against the wall as he moved. Lucas then pinned him against the bricks and delivered body blows to his side.

I got scared when Mash kneeled over, but then he stunned Lucas with an uppercut combination to the stomach and jaw. Lucas stumbled back. "I told Nadia I hate your punk ass."

Mash walked towards him and swung, knocking him down on the snow-covered rocks.

Lucas began pummeling upwards, but never landed a direct hit. Mash dug deep and began striking him over and over, then choking him until the guys pulled him off of his tired body. He broke free from their grasp and followed Lucas crawling towards the wall. He grabbed the top of a trash can, and slammed it against Lucas's limp body. "Stay the fuck away from my family!" he roared.

"Okay, Mash," said Levi, holding him back.

"Pick his arse up and get him out of here!" Mash yelled to the guards.

We came inside from the cold, shivering our asses off, and huddled near the exit while the guys packed up Mash's set. "I'm going to say this, and I mean nothing shady by it. I'm turned on, too," said Isla.

"I know right." I slapped her hand.

"He's Nadia's husband and all, but if his fine ass fought over me like he did tonight, he would be in for the ride of his life. Don't tell her I said that." Isla swore us to secrecy.

"We won't. There's enough discord in our circle."

"Mr. Security Guard might get called up to my room tonight," Isla added.

"Don't do it!" said Khai. "Then again, have fun. Just be safe."

It was the quietest we had ever been. Mash gathered us all around. "No one mention this to Nadia," he said. "I'll tell her about tonight, after the baby is born."

"How are you going to explain those cuts on your face?" I asked.

"I have cuts on my face?" His voice rose as he pressed his fingers on his cheeks, searching for gashes.

"Everyone come to my room. You, too." Isla pointed to one of the security guards.

She put her nurse skills to use, and cleaned the cuts on Mash's face. When the last bandage was taped into place, he thanked us and took advantage of our sympathy. "By chance do you girls know why Nadia laughs at the mention of hummus?"

We glanced at each other and burst into laughter. Dying to know our secret, but concerned with déjà vu, Levi interjected, "If it's anything like the California story, don't tell him."

"Should we?" Isla asked.

"Can we?" Khai asked.

"Why not?" I said. "Hummus refers to you," I answered.

"Me?"

"It's our code word to describe non-*melanated* men."

"What the hell goes on when you girls get together?" Levi asked.

Mash stared at the carpet and finally laughed.

"Wow," he said. "I'm relieved it wasn't something bad. She had me going in circles with that one."

"Good grief. You women are animals," said Brian.

"And on that note, we are turning in. Ladies, remember—breakfast in the morning. Don't be late," Khai reminded us.

"And no one tell Nadia that wanker was here." Mash repeated.

The temperature during our walk down the snow shoveled sidewalk felt as cold as it did when we were watching the brawl in the back alley. The vibe was bittersweet knowing we were about to say goodbye to Nadia once again, but would soon link up in a few months to welcome her baby.

The barista drew our faces in our beverages, humoring us by drawing Khai's head extremely big in her latte. We laughed until we cried. "I should report him to corporate. My head doesn't look like this," she fumed, and turned to give him the evil eye. He winked his eye at her and blew her a kiss, then brought complimentary scones to the table.

"I had to get your attention somehow," he said.

Khai blushed and stopped complaining.

"I see a ring on your finger. You know where to find me if that doesn't work out. You ladies have a good day." He smiled and dropped a folded napkin with his number written on it.

"You didn't see that coming, did you?" I said.

"You didn't see last night coming," Khai shot back at me.

"What did she do?" Nadia asked.

"Nothing but talk, thanks to your snitch. And before you lose your cool, you'll be happy to know Yohan and I called it quits last night."

"Thank God!" Nadia testified. "I am relieved. Now can one of you tell me why my husband came to me bruised last night?"

"No, but we can tell you he knows what hummus means."

Nadia's face went blank, and her cheeks turned redder than when we were outside in the cold. "Who blabbed?"

"We all did."

"Well, that would explain why he was grinning from ear to ear when he got in. But none of you saw the commotion last night? Mash has a nick on his lip and bruises on his chest, but only wanted to talk about how bad the other guy looked."

Isla chuckled to herself. "I'm prying here. Did you get turned on seeing him like that?"

Nadia giggled. "How did we miss Isla has a fascination with boxers? Who knew?" she teased.

"And security guards," I told.

Chapter 26
Mash

The exhaustion from traveling and working on the road prepared me for when the baby was born. Levi warned me, "This is only the beginning of feeling exhausted all the time." I had no idea how it could get worse, but remembered to take heed.

The week of the due date fast approached, and I was surrounded by women. Mrs. Melton flew in from the states, and my mother from Italy. Our little family finally came together as one, and the love and energy was so infectious, it extended to my father.

It was the first time he and my mother were in a room together since I was a child. To my surprise, time had healed their wounds. They were civil to one another — uncontrived even -- and it was secretly what I wanted all of my life. "Your mother is still quite the head turner, son." Senior tried to rekindle their old flame.

"You're looking well, Senior," my mother replied.

"May I?" he asked.

"Sure," my mother responded, giving him her cheek to kiss.

"This boy finally made us old," said my father, *scruffing* my hair.

"Yes, he has. I've been waiting on this day for a long time. The suspense of whether it's a boy or a girl keeps me up at night. My son is finally giving me a bambino." My mother beamed and pinched my cheeks.

"How was New York?" I asked Senior.

"New York went smoothly. No need to ever go back," he answered.

"Good to hear." I shook his hand. "I'll let you two catch up. We should be eating soon." I excused myself.

For the first time since we wed, The Sharpers had a family dinner at an actual dining table. I sat at the head, and spoke of the changes I noticed in Nadia over the past few months. How she was less concerned about others or their opinions. How she had become more assertive and direct, calm, quiet and reserved. How she came into her own.

The veins in her temple moved so much, it was like watching her think from the outside. Then everyone laughed when I teased about how off balance she was the past month. She was ready to have the baby, and I was ready to meet the perfect reflection of us.

The excitement from the dinner helped get the ball rolling as a trickle of water shot down her leg before she made it to the loo. Mother Melton and I rode together to the hospital. My parents followed.

The closer the contractions, the stronger Nadia's grip cradled my hands. "Is there anything I can do?" I asked.

"Call my grandmother," she demanded.

Grams answered, "Is it time?"

"Yes, ma'am," I replied. "I hope to send you a picture shortly."

"How is my gal?"

"She's doing good."

"Put her on speaker!" Nadia yelled. "Grams, I'm never having sex again."

"Oh yeah. It's time alright." Grams laughed. "Stop lying to yourself. That boy is so good looking you'll be back in there with another one next year. It's going to be alright."

The nursing staff turned their backs to Nadia and laughed at Gram's humor, but the chuckles came to an end as the minutes turned to hours, waiting for the baby to make its grand entrance.

Watching Nadia in pain was agonizing. Mother Melton couldn't bear to see her like that, and took a break to check on my mother, while I stayed by her side, having the blood squeezed from my fingers.

Her breathing intensified when she let go of my hand. The screeching noise of her nails digging into the bed made my skin crawl. I stood and kissed her forehead. "Baby, you are doing great," I said for comfort.

"How would you know!" she yelled at me like the devil.

My eyebrows raised as her voice changed from the sweet melody that once serenaded me into a deep, salty baritone. The nurse buzzed for the doctor holding in her laughter and patted me on the back.

"I'm sorry," Nadia said, and reached for my hand. "I don't know why I'm being mean to you."

"Woman, you have held grudges against me longer than anyone I know. I can take it." I assured her.

"This is not the time to remind me of my flaws," she reprimanded me, out of breath with unhappiness spread across her face.

"What I'm saying is I'm not going anywhere."

"I want to bloody cry and scream right now," she said as a tear fell from the corner of her eye.

I wiped her tears as she wept, kissing her cheeks each time one fell, then smiled at the fact she used my slang to express herself. "Did I say something to amuse you?" she fussed.

"You said bloody."

"Did I?"

I nodded.

"Well, I'm bloody miserable right now!" she cried. "I'm scared."

"So am I, but did I let you drown?"

"No," she whimpered.

"Can't you swim like a fish now?"

"Yes!" She ugly cried and smiled simultaneously.

"She's crowning," the doctor announced.

"It's time, Sweets."

She pushed and pushed. Her sweaty palms gripped around my hands, and her neck rumpled and rucked from the strain. We were almost there but not quite enough. She rested her head back against the pillow, and I wiped her forehead with my palm, brushing the flyaway hairs from the side of her face. "How are we doing, lamb chop?" I asked.

She rolled her eyes at me. "How many more times do I have to push?" she asked.

"Give me a really good push this time, and it might be the last one," the doctor answered.

With everything Nadia had left in her, she pushed a few more times, and I witnessed my daughter slide into the hands of the doctor, covered in red and dark colored goop. I cut the cord and observed everything the staff did with my little bambino at the foot of the bed. The checking of her vitals and the cleaning of her eyes, nose, and mouth.

She cried as they wrapped her in a blanket and passed her to Nadia. "Look what we did," I whispered in Nadia's ear, then kissed her on her sweet lips, as she lied there half awake.

"Congratulations on your daughter," said the doctor. "You two have one beautiful kid."

"Is she beautiful?" Nadia asked near asleep.

"Like her mother," I said. "How are you feeling?"

"I just want to hold her for a minute then go to sleep." Her voice shook.

I snapped her picture then sent it to our parents and Grams. "She's so tiny. I don't see me anywhere in her little face. She looks like your mom— and you. Where am I, little girl?" Nadia teased her while circling her cheek with her finger.

"Do you want me to bring our parents in?"

She nodded.

I had my orders but found it hard to leave their side. "Why are you still standing there?" Nadia asked.

"I know it's just down the hall, but I can't move. I don't want to leave you two," I admitted.

"I love you. You know that? Now go get our parents. Please."

I directed everyone to the wash station, then led them to the room. Nadia appeared to be resting with our baby lying on her chest. Mother Melton went over to her daughter and kissed her cheek. Nadia leered, "Look what we made," she said, then signaled for me to pick up my baby girl.

I held her in my arms, ready to protect her from the world. Her little hand wrapped around my finger, then she opened her brandy colored eyes. The most beautiful baby in the world, and she was mine. I leaned down to smell the new life scent on her skin, and presented her to the people who came before us.

"Everyone. Meet Cassia Pilara Sharper."

Thank you for diving into my fictional worlds. This Christmas my ensemble casts collide in a Mashup Novelette to celebrate love during the holidays. The On Track But Off Course Series meets The Hummus Series in, 'Levi & Launa Find Love'.

REVIEWS ENCOURAGE VORACIOUS INTEREST EVERY WHERE TO SUPPORT

ME, THE AUTHOR

I GREATLY APPRECIATE IT

XOXO

Other Books by T.K. Richards

Thank you for following the love story of Nadia and Maximus. For a bonus chapter, Second Honeymoon, following books one and two, please subscribe to: https://tkrichardsnewsletter.ck.page

The On Track but Off Course Series:
Straight Line
Derailed
The Crossing
The Perfect Gift Anthology: Mikki & Mason
The Vampiress
En Route to Emery
Juke
Can't Quit You
Still Not Over You
Love Interrupted
Levi & Launa Find Love
Playing Secret Santa

Acknowledgments

Thank you to the following people for spreading the word about my work, promoting it on social media, purchasing my books as gifts, helping me in any way I have needed assistance, and being a listening ear as I pursue this lonely, challenging career:

Mia Lindler
Kimberly Hunt of Revision Division
Racquel Henry of The Writer's Atelier
Kelly Lycurgus of Diverse Reading
Valencia Washington
Monica Manigault
Ashley Rowe

Also By T.K. RICHARDS

More Top Selling Romance by T.K. Richards

The Vampiress

Juke: A Love Story

T.K. RICHARDS is a multi-genre author of women's fiction and romance, featuring popular novels and novellas in Black Romance, Interracial/Multicultural Romance, Paranormal Romance, and YA Fiction. You can find her serialized fiction work on the Kindle Vella app. A graduate of Limestone University, T.K. has honors in Expository Writing, and was also the Poet Laureate of her graduating class. When she is not writing, she is immersed in the world of tennis, and binge watching movies—mostly comedy as she loves to laugh.

For more information about **T.K. Richards**, visit her website at www.tkrichards.com or subscribe to her newsletter at: https://tkrichardsnewsletter.ck.page

You can follow T.K. RICHARDS on the platforms listed below to interact with her personally:

facebook.com/Tkrichards

twitter.com/tkrichards1

instagram.com/t.k.richards

pinterest.com/TKWrites

tiktok.com/@tkrwrites

youtube.com/tkrichards

goodreads.com/T.k.richards

bookbub.com/authors/t-k-richards

amazon.com/author/Tkrichards

www.ingramcontent.com/pod-product-compliance
Lightning Source LLC
Chambersburg PA
CBHW011213190726
48288CB00013B/3427